D

De

Death
by
Demo

A HOME RENOVATION MYSTERY

Callie Carpenter

**CROOKED
LANE**

NEW YORK

Published in the United States by Crooked Lane Books, an imprint of The Quick Brown Fox & Company LLC.

Crooked Lane Books and its logo are trademarks of The Quick Brown Fox & Company LLC.

Library of Congress Catalog-in-Publication data available upon request.

ISBN (hardcover): 978-1-63910-562-5
ISBN (ebook): 978-1-63910-563-2

Cover design by Ben Perini

Printed in the United States.

www.crookedlanebooks.com

Crooked Lane Books
34 West 27th St., 10th Floor
New York, NY 10001

First Edition: December 2023

10 9 8 7 6 5 4 3 2 1

To all the dads who take the time to pass
their knowledge of woodworking on
to their daughters. And a special nod to
my late father, who, when I was five
years old, taught me to always sand with
the grain.

Chapter One

The house was everything she'd thought it would be. It was everything she'd remembered, everything she'd been dreaming about.
And it was all bad.

"Worse than bad," she muttered.

"Excuse me?"

Jaime Moore ignored the question, which had come from the
rumpled attorney standing next to her. From the top of his balding
head to his scuffed and untied Oxford shoes, Roger Goodwin was a
hot mess, and the only reason Jaime was still using him as her attorney
was because he'd been her dad's best friend for decades. Well, that,
and his hourly rate was the lowest in Perkins County, North Carolina.

Roger shifted his significant weight from one foot to the other.
"You're not still mad about the divorce settlement, are you?"

Of course she was. How on earth could the settlement have given
her ex-husband full ownership of King Contractors, their construction/
interior design business; all the business assets; and the gorgeous house
she'd just finished decorating, the house she'd thought would be their
forever home? Yes, back in the day, she'd been young and stupid enough
to sign a prenuptial agreement, but surely a good lawyer should have
been able to squeeze more out of the deal than this dump of a house.

Roger stirred. "There was nothing I could do, you know. Nothing anyone could do, not with that prenup you signed. Oliver Wendell Holmes himself couldn't have done any better."

On some deep-down level, Jaime knew he was right. Fifteen years ago, the summer after high school graduation, she'd been so confident that Henry and Jaime would last until the stars fell from the sky that she hadn't bother to read the details of the prenup. No, she'd made goo-goo eyes at Henry while his smiling father had pushed the pile of papers across the shiny dining table, and she'd signed where she'd been told.

Young and stupid didn't begin to cover it.

Roger slapped a meaty hand to his neck. "Dang mosquitos are eating me up. Would have thought I'd be safe from them, this time of year."

Jaime ignored that, too, and wondered how long it would take for the kudzu vines that were crawling up the old house's foundation to cover her. It was late April, after all. The trees were leafed out, the grass was green, holly bushes were blooming, and she was pretty sure she'd smelled honeysuckle drifting in from somewhere. Green things were growing like crazy, so if she stood there for a week, would that do it? She'd felt stuck for months. What were a few more days if at the end of it she could be invisible? Now there was a goal that made sense. She wouldn't hear any more tsks of pity. No more speculative glances that reeked of judgment. No more fears that she'd run into Henry and . . . That Woman.

"Okay, now that you've seen the place firsthand," Roger said heartily, rubbing his palms together, "I'm sure you agree that the only thing to do is sell it. I can call a real estate agent right now. Maybe even get someone over here today to take a look and start working on a listing price. What do say we—"

She waved a hand, cutting him off. "I'm going inside."

"Oh. Ah. Well." Roger tugged at his tie. "Not sure that's wise. You can see it's a wreck. Besides, the electricity is turned off. It'll be dark in there. I mean, look at the place."

Jaime had been. She'd done nothing but look at the house since they'd arrived. She'd vaguely remembered the place as one of the many the business had purchased over the years. Henry bought old houses; then he and his crew repaired and renovated them, and she and her team transformed them into homes, with paint, cabinetry, built-ins, fixtures, and furnishings. Only once had Henry made a mistake and bought a house that wasn't worth saving. Once. And wouldn't you know, that had been the house Henry had let her keep after the divorce.

"I don't have to do this," he'd told her last week in his attorney's gleaming office. "But I suppose it's fair that you get something."

Fair, he'd said. And he'd actually smiled when he'd said it.

She stared at the house, willing her jaw to unclench. From here she couldn't see the cracks in the foundation, but she knew they were there. She also couldn't see the termite-weakened floor joists, the leaky roof, the ancient pipes, or the heat runs wrapped with asbestos, all of which had contributed to Henry's eventual decision to pass on renovations and look for a buyer. Just her luck that she'd discovered he was cheating on her before it sold.

"So very lucky," she said. Apparently louder than she'd intended, because Roger gave her a startled look.

"What's that?" he asked. "Well, ah, sure, I suppose there's luck involved. It'll take some doing to get a real estate agent out here in the first place."

Jaime shook her head and didn't bother explaining. "I'm going in," she repeated, and started up the driveway, paying no attention to Roger's sputtering objections and outright warnings.

They'd driven separately, and both had parked at the street. They'd had to, really, because the driveway was blocked by a fallen oak tree.

Recently fallen, Jaime noted, given that the leaves were still mostly green. The tree's mass had blocked their view of the house, which was probably a good thing, because if she'd seen what the tree had done to the roof of the wraparound porch, she might never have left her ancient pickup truck.

"Good lord almighty," Roger said breathlessly, huffing and puffing as he trailed along in her wake. "I had no idea the tree hit the house. Henry didn't say a thing about the damage last week."

Of course he didn't. Jaime's jaw muscles ached from being held so tight for so long. The rat fink didn't say anything he didn't have to except when he was charming clients, contractors, and other women. Then he was all smiles and charisma.

She adjusted her baseball cap and took quick stock of the tree-induced damage. The porch roof was a complete loss; the porch railing, the same. The floor and front steps might be salvageable. Maybe.

With the tree gone, though, she could see the entire front elevation of the house. Two full stories. A turret. No, make that two turrets. Brick chimneys. A third floor with enough windows to guarantee generous attic space; clapboard siding; and so much gingerbread trim that she almost expected to see Hansel and Gretel.

"That roof is in rough shape," Roger said encouragingly. "And I see at least three broken windows from here. Who knows how many others there are? Really, Jaime, the smart thing to do is sell. With that profit and the small amount of cash you have, you can . . . ah . . . you can start fresh. Just look at it. It's massive—far too big a project for you to tackle—and with all those windows and all that fancy trim, it's an out-of-date Victorian monstrosity."

"Queen Anne," she said absently.

"What's that? Ah. Well, anyway, some sort of historic house. Probably on somebody's protected list, so that's going to make renovations even more expensive. Sweetheart, I'm just looking out for you. Your parents asked me . . . well, they know you've been having a hard time. They just want to make things easier for you."

Her parents wanted her to stop sleeping on her best friend's couch and move back to their house, which meant a return to the childhood bedroom where she'd spent so many hours spinning fantasies about the life Henry and Jaime would lead in their happily ever after. Even worse, back to the sampler her seven-year-old self had embroidered—badly—with the family's unofficial motto and that her father had framed and hung in the kitchen: "A Moore doesn't give up."

Move back? Not a chance. Not this side of the Mississippi.

"I'm going in," she said for the third time.

Roger sighed, dug into his pants pocket, and handed her two battered keys, fastened together with a paper clip. "Do you want the honors, or do you want me to—"

Jaime plucked the keys from his hand and approached the house across grass that wasn't quite tall enough to get complaints from the neighbors, not that there were any houses within a hundred yards. She climbed the front steps, avoiding a tree-damaged plank, and maneuvered around the branches, leaves, and twigs that carpeted the porch floor.

The front door was tall and wide, with wavy glass above and intricate panels below. Jaime squinted at the rusty and ornate door handle, found the slot, and eyed the keys, which were a lot like the house— worn down on all edges.

"I know just how you feel," she muttered, and shoved a key into the lock. It didn't turn. Naturally. Wordlessly, she extracted the first key, inserted the second, and this time there was a teensy bit of movement. She jiggled the handle and gave the whole thing a shove with her shoulder.

The door flew open, and her first impression was . . . light.

So much light.

Sunshine streamed in from the windows to the right, from the windows to the left, from the stairway in front of her, and through the door she'd just opened. She blinked at the unexpected brightness and wandered through the foyer and into what had surely been called a parlor.

Hardwood floor. Plaster walls. Curved windows. Interior wooden half shutters. Corniced and coffered ceiling. Marble fireplace. Dentil door trim. Period light fixtures.

A bit dazed, she walked aimlessly from spacious room to spacious room. "These ceilings have to be fourteen feet high," she murmured.

"What?" Roger asked, coming up behind her. "Oh. Ah. Could be, could be. But it all needs replastering, rewiring, replumbing, all those expensive *re* things. Taking on a project this size without a full construction crew on staff would be ridiculous."

Four main rooms in all, downstairs: parlor, kitchen, library, dining room, plus a half bath tucked until the stairs. She made the circuit again, the second time around noticing a few more details—a narrow closet between the library and dining room, the complete lack of anything in the kitchen, and the bare bulb that was the only lighting in the entire stairway.

Jaime climbed the switchback stairs and examined each of the four bedrooms and the single bathroom. Then, leaving Roger behind, she climbed a set of narrow stairs to the third floor, a space that was warm even on the cool April day. As expected, it was an unfinished attic, with piles of a hundred years of household castoffs tucked into every corner. She crossed the dusty floorboards and took in the view from the arched turret windows.

A vast expanse of green stretched out and away. Grass and trees. Plus a pond. Was that hers? Farther in the distance, a river. Beyond that, almost out of view, the rooftops of the town's skyline.

She knew she had to make a decision about the house. But it was a big thing to decide, and she was out of practice. She didn't count the divorce as a decision—that had been more an inevitable consequence of Harry's cheating on her—so this was the biggest choice she'd faced in years.

Now that she'd seen the house up close and personal, she understood why Harry had bought it in the first place. It had fantastic bones and would be glorious if restored. She didn't have to close her eyes to see the gleaming floors, the shining light fixtures, and the bright exterior colors—it was all there inside her head. But she also understood why Harry had wanted to sell. Too much work and too many unknowns for the return on investment.

"Jaime?" Roger's voice trickled up. "How long are you going to be up there? I have an appointment in half an hour."

She turned away from the window and wandered back across the attic, past ancient trunks; past the ugliest lamp she'd ever seen; past a roll-top desk that could never have fit up those stairs; past piles of boxes, heaps of magazines, and—

"Well, hello," she said, crouching down. "What are you doing down there?"

Peering up at her was a ceramic rabbit figurine, half the size of her fist, wearing a tuxedo. Gently, she brushed cobwebs from the unblinking glass eyes and studied the first thing she'd seen in the house that gave any hint of personality.

A butler, that's what he was. Sitting up tall, ears alert, competent and resourceful.

Jaime smiled at him. Butler-like, he didn't react. Didn't even blink.

Who had put the little guy between those two boxes? A child who'd been told it was time to put away childish things? Had it been put there during a rainy-day game and abandoned? Or had he been dropped, and someone used their foot to push him between the boxes, simply swept him aside?

Jaime picked up the ceramic figure and slid it into her jacket pocket. No way was she going to leave him up here all by himself.

Thinking hard and fast, she came downstairs.

"You're smiling." Roger sounded surprised. "Ah. Good. You've decided, then. Excellent. Where's my cell phone? I think there's reception here. Yes, got a couple of bars. I'll call my real estate agent and—"

"No." Jaime spoke quietly and firmly.

"Sorry?" Roger asked, cell in hand. "Ah. Well, if you have your own agent, that's fine."

"No," she said again, and this time the word sparked a feeling in her, a feeling she'd almost forgotten. The last time she could remember having felt like this was in the early years of Henry and Jaime's King Contractors, when everything had been brand new. When everything was still possible.

For the first time in months, she felt something other than misery. Something other than pure rage. It wasn't happiness; there was no possibility of being close to that—not yet. And it wasn't a returning sense of humor, although once or twice in the last week she'd felt flickers of laughter, which she was taking as a good omen. It also wasn't excitement, contentment, enjoyment, or satisfaction. But she was feeling . . . something.

Something good.

"No real estate agent," she said. "At least not until I finish this house."

Jaime tuned out Roger's blustering protests and felt a wide smile spread across her face. She'd identified the unfamiliar feeling. It was Pandora's leftover.

Hope.

Chapter Two

"You're nuts," Lara said flatly.

Jaime nodded at her best friend. "Completely possible."

"And by nuts," Lara went on, "I mean *Looney Tunes* nuts. You've taken on a lot of insane projects, and they've always turned out—I give you that—but this is beyond insanity."

"You think I can't do it?" Jaime squinted at the house. What should come first, roof repairs or replacing the termite-damaged floor joists? Hard to decide between keeping the place from falling down and keeping the place from falling down. It was two weeks after she'd been here with Roger, and though she'd busted her hind end—the oak tree was gone, the porch floor repaired, and the broken windowpanes repaired—the place didn't actually look any better. Worse, if it was possible, now that the fallen tree wasn't hiding half the house.

Lara let out a gust of air. "You can do anything you put your mind to. I'm just worried you'll work yourself into an early grave in the process."

"How kind of you to be concerned."

"Well, sort of. Mostly I want to make sure you live long enough to show Henry King what a mistake he made."

Roughly halfway between Jaime's appendix and collarbone, she felt a bubble of laughter swell, grow, then fade away. She smiled. "Good to know you have my back."

"That's what blood oaths are all about."

Twenty-four summers earlier, the Trotter family, which included the already beautiful eight-year-old Lara, had moved in next door to the Moore family. At that point the eight-year-old Jaime had had knobby knees, skinny white chicken legs, freckles, and dirty-blond hair always in need of combing.

After a few days of spying from her treehouse, Jaime saw that the new girl was everything she wasn't and could do everything she couldn't. She knew the right things to say to adults, knew how to dress so that people wouldn't make fun of her, and even knew how to bounce a basketball without it running away down the driveway. It was clear to Jaime that the new girl was going to fit in with the popular girls and wouldn't be interested in being friends with her.

So she continued to stay up in the treehouse, reading library books, reading her own books, rereading the comic books left behind by one of her brothers, and ignoring her mother's pleas to meet Lara. Then, one afternoon, she heard someone climbing the tree. A few seconds later, a curly black-haired head popped into view.

"Hi. I'm Lara. Your mom said you were up here. Do you know how to play basketball?"

"No."

"Oh. Well, do you want to learn?"

"Not really." Jaime had no interest in sports involving things that could hit her in the face and smash her glasses, an event that would render her essentially sightless.

"Oh. Okay."

The head descended, then came back up. "What are you reading?"

Jaime looked at the book's cover. "Goosebumps," she said, and went back to reading.

"Which one?"

"Um." Jaime looked at the cover again. "*Werewolf of Fever Swamp*."

"That's a good one." Lara nodded. "I like *Curse of the Mummy Tomb* the best. So far, anyway. I haven't read all of them. Have you?"

"Yeah," Jaime said. "My grandmother sends them to me."

"You own them all?" Lara's eyes opened wide.

Five minutes later, they were in Jaime's bedroom, deep in a discussion that had basically never stopped. At the end of the summer, they pricked their palms with safety pins and shook hands, sealing their friendship with a light smear of blood and vowing to always tell each other everything.

And mostly they had. Their relationship drifted a bit after high school, when Lara went off to college and graduate school, and when Jaime married Henry, but it all came back stronger than ever when Lara returned to Green River, taking a job with one of the big Charlotte banks. If Lara hadn't been around to pick up Jaime's sobbing bits and pieces after the day she'd walked in on her former husband's infidelity, now known as "That Day," Jaime was pretty sure she'd still be a sodden puddle of sorrow.

Now, Jaime gave Lara a look of affection. "I have to start doing something soon, or I'll end up sleeping on your couch the rest of my life. Not sure Tony will be okay with that."

Lara disregarded her fiancé's concerns with an airy twiddle of her fingers. "He understands. And I'm at his place most of the time anyway, so it's not a problem."

But someday it would be, Jaime knew. She'd put off making decisions about her future until the divorce settlement was final. And now it was.

She felt her molars grind.

Breathe, she told herself. *Breathe and focus on what's in front of you.*

Since what was in front of her was the dilapidated mess bestowed on her by her ex-husband, the sight wasn't exactly calming.

"Come on," she told Lara. "Don't worry—it's safe enough."

"Safe for now," was what the structural engineer she'd hired had said. "It's not going to fall down today, or even tomorrow," he'd told her. "But if you want to save the place, there's a lot that needs to happen soon."

Like that was something she didn't know. In the fourteen years she'd been part of King Contractors, she'd been condescended to by men from the age of eighty down to eighteen. When she'd fumed about it to Henry, he'd laughed and told her to use it to her advantage. Unfortunately, she'd never known how to do that.

"It's perfectly safe," she said, climbing the steps to the porch. She jumped up and down. "See? Not a single creak."

"Easy for you to say." Hesitantly, Lara went up one step. "You weigh a fraction of me."

"Stop being such a scaredy cat and get up here. I want your help, and the day's half over."

Lara reached the porch proper and squinted at the trees surrounding the house. "That yellow disc up there, that bright one that isn't above the trees yet, says different."

"Okay, maybe only a quarter over. Still, the sooner you help me do this, the sooner I can get off your couch and move in here. And quit saying you're fine if I stay forever. I love you for that, but it's not a long-term solution."

Jaime unlocked the front door and waved Lara inside. "The electricity was turned on last week, so all the light switches work. Go on in. I need to get some things." She hurried down the steps and over to her truck, where she grabbed a lumpy plastic grocery bag and her morning purchase from the hardware store, bought two minutes after the place opened.

Back inside, she put the heavy part of the tool on the floor and leaned its long handle against a wall between the library and the dining room.

"Um, question?"

Jaime followed the sound of Lara's voice and found her in the kitchen. Or what would eventually be a kitchen. She had plans for it to be a gorgeous sun-filled space with a large island and an eating nook. All that was in the distant future, though, because the cavernous room was currently nothing but walls, floors, and bare windows. Its only redeeming feature was a single built-in oak cabinet toward the back of the room with tall glass doors above waist-high, paneled doors below.

"What's up?" she asked. But as soon as the question came out, she realized what had happened. "There's a simple explanation," she said quickly.

"Really?" Lara stared meaningfully at the one thing in the kitchen— a bag of cat food—and raised her eyebrows. "Because this certainly looks like you have a cat. The woman who has always said she doesn't care for cats, who won't even watch kitten videos, now has a cat?"

"No, I don't," Jamie said. "Last week, it just . . . showed up. It wasn't here, then it was. I'm sure it has a home somewhere. I'm just feeding it until its owner shows up." She saw the corner of Lara's mouth twitching and held out the plastic bag. "Here. Take the glasses."

Lara peered in. "Little early in the day, isn't it?" She pulled out two plastic champagne flutes.

"Yes. But we couldn't do this last night because you and Tony went to that blue grass concert." Jamie took hold of the champagne bottle and shoved the empty plastic bag into a pocket of her work pants, right next to the Swiss Army knife she always carried with her on a job site. "And I want to do it before I take the first swing."

"It's going to bubble all over," Lara warned.

Jaime didn't see that as a problem. The flooring was on the demolish list, and the champagne was cheap. She wiggled the stopper and felt more then heard a slight pop.

"Got it!" Lara held her flute under the cascading dribble. "Okay, fill 'er up . . . now yours . . . done. Who's making the toast?" After a pause, during which Jaime looked mostly at her champagne, Lara said, "Luckily, I have a speech all prepared."

But Jaime knew that was a lie. She had such a deep fear of public speaking that even a short speech with only one person in attendance could turn her stomach into a mass of knots. "Go on," she said. "Things to do here, remember?"

"To this house, which has immense potential." Lara held up her plastic flute. "But more than that, to Jaime Moore, who is the bravest person I know."

Jaime's eyes misted, which wouldn't do. Not at all. "And," she said, so quickly that her tummy wouldn't know what had happened to it, "to my new favorite tool, all twelve pounds of it."

They solemnly clicked rims and sipped.

Lara made a face "This stuff is awful." She rubbed her mouth with the back of her hand.

"Well, it was more the gesture." Since the kitchen lacked anything as fancy as a working sink, Jamie opened the kitchen window and tossed the pale liquid out in a long swoosh. She could do this easily because, like in every movie and TV show ever made—but basically never in modern life—there was no screen. "Ready?"

Lara defenestrated her own champagne. They left the flutes on the floor and traipsed back to the dining room, where Lara took out her phone and tapped on the movie app. "You're sure about taking this wall down?" she asked.

"Don't you start." Jamie's mouth tightened into a firm line as she cast a practiced eye over the wall that cut the proportions from a room with space for a generously sized dining table with chairs all around, to a narrow room with proportions that made her skin crawl. "I know what I'm doing."

"And don't *you* start." Lara rolled her eyes. "I'm not questioning your knowledge, your abilities, or your vision. You have tons of that."

"Oh." She reached for her tool belt, which she'd left on the broken newel post the night before, and dug around for her work gloves and safety goggles. "Good to know."

"Henry was an idiot," Lara said firmly. "He was threatened by you—that's why he kept you in the background."

Jaime shook her head. She wasn't going to think about Henry. Not today. Hopefully, not ever.

"No," Lara went on "you're right. This wall doesn't belong. Even I can tell the baseboard trim doesn't match. Whoever decided to put a deep closet here should have their head examined. What was it your dad's lawyer friend said?"

She remembered the conversation clearly. "Roger said he'd been told the wall was a later addition to the house and that it was load bearing. Had be to be put in because of the termite damage to the floor joists." Though the termite problem made her clutch, she knew there were ways to fix anything, if you had time or money. Both would be ideal, but you couldn't have everything.

"And your structural engineer said the wall could come out."

"That's what he told me." More importantly, that's what was in his written report, emailed to her first thing that morning. Immediately after reading it, she'd jumped into her truck and driven to the hardware store.

She reached down and grabbed the shiny orange fiberglass handle of the sledgehammer and eyed Lara over the top of it. "So, what's the problem?"

"Just . . ." Lara shrugged. "Once you start this, you're going to be a hundred percent emotionally vested in the project. There won't be any going back."

"Exactly." Jaime gripped the handle tight. "Stay clear."

She stood strong and firm, feet wide, knees slightly bent, and took one deep breath to clear her head of sticky mental cobwebs. Another deep breath to do the same thing because the first one hadn't done its job. A final full breath because of what was about to happen. She could almost see it, the finished house in all its renovated glory, and she smiled.

As she'd done so many times over the years, she lifted the sledge over her shoulder, and very close to laughing because there was nothing as fun as demolition, she swung forward with all her might, sliding her hands close together as she aimed, leaning in to add her own weight to the blow, whipping the sledge's head around fast and hard and sure.

Crash!

The wall collapsed, spewing out a huge puff of plaster dust.

Jamie backed away, coughing, and wondered what had happened. Walls didn't do that. Even a cheap wall put up by a shoddy contractor wouldn't have crumbled to bits after a single hit.

Lara waved the dust away from her face. "Girl, you got more game than I realized. What are you going to do with the rest of the morning? If you get working on that world peace thing, you might have it figured out by sundown."

"Something's not right." Jaime eyed the settling plaster dust. "Walls don't come down that easy. That wall was plaster, and plaster has to stick to something. There should have been wooden lath behind it."

She looked up at the high ceiling. "Check it out," she said, pointing at the ragged edge hanging down. "That's cardboard. What kind of idiot uses cardboard to back up a plaster wall? I'm surprised the plaster stuck long enough to set. Any little bump would have cracked it."

"Well," Lara said cheerfully, "there's no accounting for people. Now what?"

Jaime toyed at the heap of plaster with the toe of her work boot and thought about all the push-broom and shovel work ahead of her. "Clean up. There's a dumpster in the back."

"Dirty work," Lara said, sighing. "You know that's not my gig."

It never had been. Jaime smiled. "Thanks for being here for the first swing." Back in her King Contractors days, she and Henry had always made a ceremony out of demolition day. That it was only herself and Lara for this particular house was just fine with her. Pretty much.

"I can stay for a little while," Lara said. "Gets me out of the Tuesday morning staff meeting."

"If you're sure, then yeah, I'll take all the help I can get." Jaime dug into her tool belt for a dust mask and her spare work gloves, which she handed to Lara. "Take these gloves. But I only have one dust mask, so stand back while I clear out some of this mess."

She waited until Lara stepped away, and then turned her attention to the heap of plaster and cardboard. Using the head of the sledge-hammer, she knocked the bits of plaster stuck to the floor away from her and into the heaping pile already created by the wall's fall from grace. Dust billowed in great clouds, but this time she kept working through it. A swing and a small crash. Swing and a crash. Swing and a thump. Swing and a—

Wait. *Thump?*

"What's the matter?" Lara asked.

"Not sure." Jaime poked at the already-large pile of rubble with the sledge. "Probably nothing." But with old houses, you never knew.

She'd found everything from old newspapers to socks inside walls. One time she'd found bottles of moonshine and—

She came to an abrupt halt. "No," she breathed. "No, no, no."

"H-holy to-tomatoes." Lara's voice, typically sure and confident, was suddenly shaky. "That's . . . that's . . ."

For the second time in six months, Jaime's world came to a crashing halt. Only this time it wasn't because of something Henry had done.

This time it was because someone else's world had ended.

"That's a dead body," she said. And slid her phone out of her pocket to call 911.

Chapter Three

The first law enforcement officer on the scene was a young man who didn't look old enough to drive. He took one look at the plaster-dusted body, swallowed, and radioed for assistance. Soon, vehicles were spilling out of the driveway and onto Holt Road. City police cars, an ambulance, sheriff's cars—even a fire truck.

Jaime and Lara, who had been consigned to the parlor, watched the comings and goings with bemusement.

"A fire truck?" Lara asked, raising one eyebrow as she posed the question. "Why on earth would a fire truck show up? An ambulance I sort of get, but a fire truck?"

Jaime squinted through the front window's wavy glass. "Maybe they have some special tool?"

"What is it with you and tools?" Lara shook her head and stood, rubbing her hips.

The upturned five-gallon paint buckets Jaime had hauled out of her pickup because she hadn't gotten around to dropping them off at recycling were not ideal for prolonged sitting. Better than nothing, but not by much.

"Having the right tool makes a job easier," Jaime said. She might have been quoting Norm Abram from *This Old House*, the home renovation show she'd watched as a toddler, but maybe it was something everyone in the skilled trades said. "Same thing with"—she searched for an equivalent idea—"cooking. You wouldn't want to use a paring knife to cut up a pumpkin, right?"

Lara didn't seem interested in Jaime's analogy. "Fire truck dudes are talking to the police dudes," she said, peering out the window. "But they're not getting out of the truck."

"Huh." Jaime shifted on her bucket and tried to summon interest in Lara's play-by-play commentary. She wanted to pay attention—she way deep down did—because otherwise she'd have to think about what her sledgehammer had done, and she'd rather avoid that for as long as possible.

Instead, she found herself thinking about the sledge she'd purchased that morning, the tool that had been, for a few short minutes, her favorite tool ever. Now, she wasn't sure she'd ever be able to use it without remembering the—

"Ms. Moore?"

Jaime looked up at the uniformed Black man standing in front of her. He was at least six feet tall, solid as a brick foundation, and looked about as serious. "Yes?" she asked, standing slowly.

"I'm Detective Scoles with the Perkins County Sheriff's Department. I'd like to ask a few questions."

"Should she have her lawyer?" Lara demanded.

The detective eyed her. "Ms. Trotter. You're Joe's sister, aren't you?"

Lara stared at him hard, then snorted a laugh. "And you're Bax Scoles."

"Baxter. That's right."

Jaime, though she'd lived her entire life in Perkins County, was still amazed at its small-town nature. After all, there were over fifty thousand county residents, and new people were moving in all the time. Yet here were Lara and the detective with only one degree of separation. Though she was mildly curious how the detective knew Joe, she was far more curious about his questions.

"Detective?" she asked. Then, not waiting for him to focus his calm dark eyes on her, she rushed ahead. "Do you know who it is? The . . . body?"

Even though the remains had looked dried and decayed, they'd been undeniably human. They had been wedged inside the wall, laid out long and turned on their side. And although Jaime been trying for the last hour, she hadn't come up with anything that looked like a human body other than a human body.

"And what happened?" Lara asked. "I mean, it's obvious that something horrible happened, but what exactly? And when? That wall is the newest thing in this place. That body, though, looks as if it's been there since Moses parted the Red Sea."

The detective half smiled. "Here I thought I'd be the one asking the questions."

"Ask away." Lara crossed her arms. "Doesn't mean we have to answer."

"We're happy to cooperate," Jaime said, giving her friend a "be-quiet-or-I'll-tell-him-about-your-speeding-habit" look. "I'm just not sure how much help we'll be. I only took possession of the house yesterday."

Detective Scoles slid a small notebook from his shirt pocket and flipped it open. "You first entered the premises two weeks ago?"

"That's right."

"But you are a part owner of King Contractors, and King Contractors bought this house three years ago."

"Former part owner," Jaime corrected. "Henry King is now sole owner."

The detective nodded and jotted a note. "Divorce?"

"I signed the final papers two weeks ago." Jaime prepared herself, waiting for a comment. When none came, she let out a breath she hadn't realized she'd been holding. She appreciated his business-like approach. After all, there was no need to offer vague murmurs of sympathy to her. This was a police investigation; better to save those murmurs for victims.

"Who in King Contractors was likely to have been inside the house?"

Jaime thought for a moment. "Henry. And Bob McNinch. He's the crew foreman and supervises all the work crews. Maybe some of the crew guys? But I really don't know. You'll have to ask Henry. He took care of purchasing the properties we worked on."

Off to her left, Jaime heard a quiet snort from Lara. For years, Lara had been telling her that she left too many decisions to Henry. And for years, Jaime had been telling her back that she was just fine with the work distribution, that she wasn't really interested in the purchasing side of things anyway.

But had that been true? Or had she gone along with Henry's decisions because it was easier?

The detective paused in his writing. "Can you think of anyone else?"

"Who's been inside?" Jaime, suddenly exhausted, rubbed her face. "I hired an engineer to assess the structural integrity." She gave him the name. "And my attorney, Roger Goodwin. I can't think of anyone else."

"Thank you, Ms. Moore. I appreciate your help." He returned the notebook to his shirt pocket. "We have your contact information. As soon as—"

"Hang on," Lara said. "That's it? A couple of questions and you're off? Don't we get to know anything?"

The detective gave her a calm look. "Unfortunately, Ms. Trotter, at this point there isn't much to know. What we have is a body of unknown gender and age, dead by means currently undetermined at a date currently undetermined."

"But—"

"We'll do our best to find answers," he said. "Until we find them, however, access to this house will be restricted to law enforcement. It's a crime scene. As I was saying, Ms. Moore, we'll contact you as soon as we have information."

Five seconds later, Jaime and Lara found themselves on the porch, staring at a front door that was closing in their faces.

"Well, that just happened," Lara said, glaring at the door, then at Jaime. "What are you going to do now?"

Jaime quickly ran through a mental list of options. Really, there was only one reasonable choice.

"We go to Betty's."

Betty's Place had been an integral part of Green River life for so many years that no one alive had ever met the original owner. The current Betty, whose name was actually Heather, had taken over from her great-aunt five years earlier, and the entire town had breathed a sigh of relief when the days passed without any changes to the downtown restaurant.

Eventually, worn chairs were replaced, paint was touched up, and the menu grew from fried chicken, collard greens, and pecan pie to include pasta dishes, salads, and (gasp!) roasted vegetables, but the process had been so gradual that the changes barely earned a mention in post-church conversations.

Jaime and Lara parked their vehicles in the rear parking lot and came in through the back door. They slid onto the vinyl seats of a booth and waved off the menus offered by a chirpy young waitress. It was too late for breakfast and too early for lunch, so they ordered coffee and a cinnamon roll to split until it was time to order real food.

"I appreciate you taking the entire day off work," Jaime said. "You didn't have to do that."

"Did too. That's what the best friend in the world does."

Jaime frowned. "How can you be the best friend in the world? Because I'm pretty sure the trophy is mine right now." It was a pseudo-contest they'd been having for almost twenty years. Somewhere along the line they'd bought a golden cup, had it engraved with "World's Best Friend," and passed it back and forth.

"It's in my apartment," Lara said. "And since you're squatting, I'm going to say possession is mine, saith the law."

"Pretty sure that's not how it works."

"Detective Scoles gave you his business card. Give him a call and ask."

The only thing Jaime wanted to hear from the detective was that she could get back to working on the house. "All dressed up and nowhere to go," she murmured.

"What? Oh, right. Not being able to work on the house is kind of a problem, isn't it?"

In all sorts of ways. Jaime stirred cream into her coffee, saw that the color wasn't quite right, and poured in a little more. "I have delays built into the schedule, but this?" She shook her head. "There's no way to predict when I'll be able to get back inside. Might be days, might be weeks."

"You'll figure it out."

Jaime looked at Lara across the twin spirals of rising coffee steam. "How is it you can sound so confident about something you basically know nothing about?"

"Because I know you." Lara grinned. "And I know that you were the one carrying King Contractors. Without you doing all the real work, Harry is going to crater. I give him two years, tops."

It was surely a character flaw that Jaime felt a deep sense of satisfaction at the notion. "Doubt it," she said. "His daddy will rescue him."

"Maybe." Lara shrugged. "Or maybe Daddy will finally recognize that his son is a—"

24

"Here you ladies go," chirped their waitress. "Fresh out of the oven."

For a brief second, Jaime and Lara admired the cinnamon roll, worthy of a TV baking show. Then they thanked the beaming waitress and picked up their forks.

"Anyway," Jaime said after she'd inhaled a bite of the gooey goodness, "none of that really matters. Okay, before you hurt yourself trying to eat and talk at the same time, yes, it matters, but whatever may or may not happen to King Contractors isn't relevant to today's problems."

Lara half nodded and kept chewing. Jaime kept talking. Working through a situation out loud usually helped her figure a way through things, even if she wasn't talking to anyone other than herself.

"The goal is to renovate the house and sell it for a nice tidy profit," she said. "My capital is limited to the cash I got out of the divorce, which was the cash I'd put into King Contractors when we started the business."

Lara nodded. "Your college fund. I remember."

So did Jaime. Her parents, both high school teachers, had been disappointed that she hadn't gone on to university, but she and Henry had been too eager to start their business. "The longer we wait," he'd said, "the more money we lose." And now here she was, back where she'd been right out of high school. Roger had won her the equivalent of fifteen years' interest, but that was a moral victory more than a financial one.

"The bank will give me a construction loan," she said, "and I've matched the payments to a combination of my free capital and time in renovation."

Lara grinned. "Look at you, talking like a financier. It's adorable."

"Like I said, I've calculated for normal delays, but this?" Jaime shook her head. "How do I adjust for a total and complete unknown?"

Lara pointed a fork at her. "We need a plan."

"We?" Jaime asked.

"Absolutely 'we,'" Lara said. "How am I ever going to get the trophy back if I don't help you with this?"

"Fair enough." She nodded. "A plan it is. But a plan for what exactly? And don't say for sneaking back into the house in the middle of the night to work on renovations, because that's not going to happen."

Lara looked at her sadly. "You are no fun."

"Never have been. So, if I can't work on the house, I see only two options. One is sit on your couch eating bonbons while I wait for the police to let me back into the house."

"Sounds like a little bit of fun."

Jaime thought it might be fun for five minutes. After that she'd be bored silly. "Option number two is to get a job."

"Working for someone else?" Lara's eyebrows went up. "You'd hate that."

She would indeed. After so many years of running her own company, she had zero inclination to subject herself to an organizational culture created by someone else.

Her parents wanted her to see this time as an opportunity. To try something different. To get that college degree. But all she'd ever wanted to do was to rescue houses and make them homes again.

Jaime touched her coat pocket, feeling the tuxedo bunny she'd wrapped in a clean paint rag before they'd been ejected from the parlor. He was her touchstone for the house, the symbol for the renovation. She'd never tell a soul—not even Lara—but when she brought the house back to life, she'd make sure Mr. Rabbit would have a place of honor.

The two women forked up the last bits of cinnamon roll.

Jamie knew she should call Roger. He not only needed to know what happened, but she should also tell him that Detective Scoles would be knocking on his door. Henry she would not be calling. No reason the arrival of the detective couldn't be a nice little surprise for him. And for That Woman.

"You know," Lara said. "There is a third option."

"Run away and join the circus?"

"And now we're up to four options. My idea is way better than yours, though."

"You sure? Because I bet my sledgehammering skills would transfer well to driving in tent stakes."

Lara ignored her. "Option number four is to figure out who that was in the house and what that person was doing there."

"I doubt Detective Scoles would take kindly to me co-opting his investigation."

"Not talking about police investigation stuff." Lara leaned forward. "I'm talking about things we have connections to. That wretched ex of yours, for one. He owes you, and he knows it. Talk to him, and I bet you learn something about what went on in that house, something that he won't tell Bax Scoles. Same with your old foreman, Bob. And Roger."

Jaime sat back, staring up at the restaurant's tin ceiling. "You know," she said slowly, "you might have something there."

"Sure I do. I'm smart, remember? And the key thing about option four is your personal investment. You're the one who cares about getting access to the house. This will be just one case of many for the sheriff's department. For you it's the thing that matters most. You'll be way more motivated than Scoles to get this resolved."

"Sure, but there's one big problem. I have no idea how do any of that. And the last thing I want to do is talk to Henry."

Lara gave her a look. "I get that, but what if it means getting back into the house sooner rather than later?"

"Then . . ." She thought about it and came to the same conclusion. "Then I need to pull up my big girl panties and figure out how."

Lara smiled and slapped the table. "Hah! That's more like it. Now we can get going on a solid strategy." She rubbed her palms together. "Let's get some lunch, then go back to my place. We'll want paper and pens and my computer, at the very least."

"Sure," Jaime said, grateful beyond measure for her friend's enthusiasm, "but there's one thing I have to do first."

"What?"

She sighed. "Feed a cat."

Chapter Four

The first appearance of the cat had been the morning Jaime explored the outbuildings. She'd expected rodents, spiders, and snakes, but hadn't been prepared for the howling ball of fur that had erupted from behind a pile of scrap wood.

In retrospect, the cat had probably been just as startled as she'd been, but at the time it had felt like a personal attack.

"Git!" she'd called, swatting at the vacant air the cat had left behind in its rush to escape Jaime's vicinity. She'd been raised with the sure knowledge that there were two kinds of people in the world—dog people and cat people—and the Moores were firmly in the dog hemisphere. Inky, the spaniel she and Henry had adopted early in the marriage, had passed away from old age just before That Day, and her death had caused Jaime more tears than the divorce had. Which should have told her volumes about the whole situation, really.

She'd watched the cat hurl itself out the shed door and fully expected to never see it again.

That same afternoon, she'd seen it slinking into the overgrown foundation bushes, and just as the last light was leaving the sky, she'd seen it tiptoe back toward the shed. "Good luck," she said with satisfaction. The door was shut and locked, and there was no way that cat would be able to get back inside.

The next morning, she unlocked the door, opened it, and started examining the pile of wood, which the day before had looked like quarter-sawn oak.

"Mmwwwwwww."

This time, the cat's low growl didn't exactly startle Jaime. More, it changed the situation from mild irritation to a declaration of war. She spent more time than she should have in a serious hunt for broken windows, gaps in foundations, and rotted siding. Nothing. Yet every morning when she arrived, the cat was back inside the shed.

"How are you getting in?" she'd yelled after it. After a week she'd come to see the cat was mostly gray, with a whiteish chest and paws and some white on its face. A mutt cat, if that was a term in the feline world.

"Mmww!" it called back.

Jaime had laughed.

It was the first time she'd laughed out loud in weeks. Months, even. She'd moved to the doorway of the shed and watched the cat gallop across the lawn, his hind end moving a teensy bit faster than his front end, as if the two ends weren't quite talking to each other.

And she laughed again.

That afternoon she stopped at the pet store and bought a food bowl, a water bowl, and a bag of cat food. She looked at the litter boxes, but figured the cat was taking care of that by itself, at least for now.

The following morning, she filled the food bowl and took it to the back porch. "I need to clear out the shed," she'd called to the cat, which she knew was hiding in the shrubbery. "It's going to be a staging location for materials, so it'll be busy in there. You're not going to like it. At all."

A small movement in the shrubbery told her that he was listening.

She shook the food bowl. "I'm going to leave this here for the day, and then, before I leave, I'll move it inside. Because I figure if you can get inside a locked shed, you can get in the house, right?"

In answer, there was a slightly less small movement of the shrubbery. She smiled, put the bowl on the top step, and went back to work.

Post-Betty's, she thought about what to do. With law enforcement and other assorted professionals crawling all over the house, there was no way the cat would come anywhere close to its food dish. Sure, he'd taken care of himself until Jaime had come along, but now that she'd started feeding him, she felt responsible for continuing the process.

Back to the shed.

She bought another round of bowls and food, and drove back to the house, where police and other intimidating vehicles were still spilling out of the driveway.

Jaime parked on the street and traipsed to the shed, keeping her distance from the house. Though Detective Scoles had said the house was a crime scene, he hadn't said anything about the rest of the grounds, so there was no reason she couldn't be there, yet somehow she felt the need to slide in and out invisibly and quickly.

The shed door creaked as she opened it, and she made a mental note to get some oil for the hinges. "Hey!" she called out in a loud whisper. "Your food will be in here for a while, okay?"

She put the bowl on the dirt floor and opened the bag of cat food.

"What are you doing?"

Jaime froze at the male voice. Not the detective. Somebody else from the sheriff's department?

She stood and turned. A man about her own age was standing just outside the shed, smiling at her. A very good-looking man. Hot, even, if you liked guys who wore flannel shirts and work boots, which Jaime had until she'd discovered that her ex-husband had been cheating on her, so she considered herself immune to the type. This guy looked vaguely familiar, but she couldn't place him. However, he clearly wasn't law enforcement, so she relaxed.

"There's a cat," she said. "Gray. Some white."

"I know that cat." He nodded. "See him around all the time. He's yours?"

"What? No, of course not." She looked at the bag of food in her hand. "I'm feeding him until I find his owner, is all. He's bound to belong to someone, right?"

The guy grinned. "You're not a cat person, are you?"

"Not even close."

"I'm Mike Darden. I live next door," he said, gesturing. "Saw all the commotion, then saw someone sneaking in here. Just wanted to make sure nothing weird was going on."

"Actually, there's a lot of weirdness going on." She stepped out into the sunlight and introduced herself, then said, "Since you live here, you might as well know," and proceeded to tell him about her morning. The wall. The sledgehammer. The body. The call to 911. The change from renovation site to crime scene.

"Huh." Mike looked at the house. "Someone has been in there, dead, and no one knew anything about it? That's . . ."

"Creepy?" she suggested.

He nodded. "Also sad."

"And mysterious."

"Lot of that," Mike said. "Plus, it's bound to throw a huge wrench into your renovation plans."

"Yeah, well." She shrugged. "I'm working on a plan for that."

"Hope it works out. I've always liked this house."

"Thanks." The bag of cat food was growing heavier, so Jaime shifted it from one hand to the other. "Thanks for keeping an eye on the place. I appreciate it."

"No problem. Small towns, neighbors, all that." He gave her a warm smile.

"Sure." Jaime inched away. "It was nice meeting you, but now I really have to get going. Plans to adjust. All that." She nodded and headed back across the lengthening lawn to her pickup truck.

"One suggestion?" Mike called after her. "You might think about giving that cat a name."

*   *   *

"I'm not naming the cat," Jaime told Lara.

"Okay, you're not."

"And how does Mike Darden know it doesn't belong to someone? There are all sorts of reasons why it ended up in that shed."

"Yeah?"

"Absolutely," Jaime said, then tried to think of one. "Um, it could have wandered off and not found its way home. Or it could have accidentally been locked outside of its house and picked up by someone who thought it didn't have a home, but it struggled free and is still trying to find its way back to its owners." She found the story unlikely but compelling, and just pathetic enough to make her the teensiest sniffly.

"Mmm."

Jaime sat up. "You're not actually listening to me, are you?"

"Nope."

They were in Lara's apartment in their usual spots. Jaime was on the couch, which would in the course of a few hours turn into her bed, and Lara was sitting at the table that served as dining area and home office. Lara had been leasing the same one-bedroom space since she'd come home after graduate school. Technically, she could have afforded something bigger and nicer, but she wanted to pay off her multitude of student loans as quickly as possible, so small and worn it was.

Jaime hauled herself up off the couch and stretched. "What are you doing?"

"Told you. Working out a plan."

"And I told you I already have one."

Lara took a hand off her computer's keyboard and held up her index finger. "One is not enough. You should have this many." She held her hand open, displaying all five digits. "Besides, your plan sucks."

There was some truth in that because Jaime's plan in its entirety was: Talk To People and See What I Can Find Out. She peered over Lara's shoulder and wasn't surprised to see a spreadsheet on the laptop's screen. It was multi-tabbed, with filters, and for all she knew, also included graphs and array formulas. "Graduate school ruined you."

"Tell that to my diploma." Lara tapped a few more keystrokes, then sat back and flexed her fingers, cracking her knuckles. "Okay, take a look. Let me know what you think."

"I think you're wacko. I appreciate your help and all—I really do—but do you really think I'm going to what, track my progress with a spreadsheet?"

She could, of course. Tracking was what she'd done for every job King Contractors had ever taken on. She'd done it quietly because Henry hadn't wanted to do anything that felt like bureaucracy, but her charts had saved the day multiple times. This time, though, she wasn't sure she saw the point.

"Don't be stupid," Lara said. "You do the real work; I'll do the easy stuff of updating the spreadsheet."

"Since you put it like that." Jaime sat in the other chair and pulled the laptop toward her. Her face started squinching itself as she read. "Why are there so many things on here that I don't want to do?"

"Because you're a home renovator, not an investigator."

"Well, there you go."

"But it doesn't matter." Lara stood, went to the refrigerator, and poured two glasses of sweet tea from a pitcher. "Doing some amateur investigating is the only way to be proactive about getting back into the house."

Jaime knew that. She just didn't like it. "Why are the things we don't want to do always the things we need to do?"

"Because if we wanted to do them, they'd already be done." She held out a glass. "Sad fact of life."

Jaime took a long sip of tea and gestured at the computer. "Can you rate the tasks in terms of importance?" Because some of them wouldn't be too horrible, really. It would be easy enough to call Roger. She should have done that already. And she wouldn't mind talking to Bob McNinch. She'd been the one to hire him as crew foreman in the first place, and they'd always had a good working relationship.

"Only with hindsight. Right now, there's no way of knowing. That's why I created five different strategies. Each starts the same way, then deviates depending on what you learn from each task."

Jaime poked around on the computer. "All of these plans start with me talking to Henry? Seriously?"

"Who else would you talk to first, other than Roger and your parents?" She glanced over. "Hang on. I know that look. You have got to be kidding me."

"It's just that . . ." Jaime squirmed. "I know what Mom and Dad are going to say. They'll take this as one more reason for me to move home and have them help me figure out what I want to do with the rest of my life."

"You know how dumb that is, right? They're going to find out, one way or another, and it's going to make things worse if they find out from someone else."

Jaime knew all that—of course she did. Still, the knowing didn't seem to be pushing her to pick up the phone and call.

"Here." Lara picked up Jaime's phone from the coffee table and tossed it to her. "I have to scoot," she said, grabbing her purse. "Tony and I are meeting some of his work friends for dinner, and I'm already late. Call your parents," she said, opening the apartment door. "If you contact anyone else, text me the results. The spreadsheet is in the Cloud. I can keep it updated from my phone."

The efficiency of Jaime's best friend never ceased to amaze her. "Have a good"—the door closed—"time."

She dug her phone out of the side pocket of her work pants and laid it face up on the table, put her index finger at one corner, and thought about the rules for her latest decision-making matrix.

"Home button at the bottom," she said out loud, "and I'll call Mom. Home button at the top, I'll call Henry. To the right, I'll call Roger. To the left, Bob."

She gave the phone a hard clockwise spin and put her hands in her lap, because it would be cheating if she touched it before it came to a complete stop.

"Round and round and round it goes," she chanted softly, "and where it stops, nobody knows." She couldn't remember the first time she'd used her phone as a tool for making decisions, but it had been long enough ago that she'd been embarrassed to tell anyone what she was really doing when she spun her phone, and now keeping the action to herself was an ingrained habit.

But the rules didn't preclude her wishing for a certain stop position, so she focused all her attention on hoping for a horizontal end to the spin. Either Roger or Bob would be fine. But she had absolutely no desire to call either her parents or Henry. Not today. Tomorrow, maybe. After a good night's sleep.

Or two.

The phone's spin slowed, then came to a complete halt. Not vertical, not horizontal. Jaime stood and examined it from a straight-down view, the better to judge the angle accurately.

"Forty-one," she murmured, nodding. She had no idea where the ability to judge angles within a degree or two came from, but it did come in handy. Henry had often joked it was a pity there was no way to monetize the skill.

And since it was forty-one degrees away from the horizontal home button to the right, by the rules of the game, she now had to call Roger.

"Sometimes things just work out," she said, tapping Roger's name from her Favorites list.

"Well, hello, Jaime," he answered. "To what do I owe the pleasure? If you changed your mind about selling the house, we can get it listed tomorrow."

"No. I need to tell you something," she said. "Are you sitting down?"

"Well, that sounds like bad news. Hold on. I'm driving. Let me pull over here—just a second, I have to . . . there we go. Now," he said, and Jaime heard the *thunk* of a transmission sliding into Park, "what can I do for my favorite client?"

She almost smiled. Every client of Roger's was his favorite. "It's about the house," she said. "I was out there with Lara this morning, to take a swing at that wall—you know, that new one that didn't belong, and—"

"Jaime Evelyn Moore," he thundered. "Tell me you didn't take it down. That was a load-bearing wall. The whole house could be in danger of collapse!"

She bit her tongue. Literally. How was it that so many people didn't understand how houses worked? Even if that wall had been load bearing, there were ways to safely deal with its removal. There were these things called steel I beams, which had been around for more than a hundred years, that would do the trick nicely.

"I had a structural engineer take a look," she said. "He went into the crawl space and the attic, checking the soundness of the structural beams and joists, and said there was nothing structural about that wall." She paused, then said, "I can send you the report, if you want. There are calculations for every room. Lots of numbers. The full report is nearly twenty pages long."

"Ah. Well, no need for that."

Of course there wouldn't be. Jaime knew Roger had spent much of his adult life avoiding anything that resembled math.

"What engineer?" Roger asked. "You made sure he's licensed, didn't you?"

Sometimes Roger acted more like her dad than her dad did. "Yes," she said, giving the engineer's name, which meant nothing to Roger since the guy worked mostly in Charlotte on big commercial projects.

"I suppose it'll be okay," Roger said grudgingly.

"Anyway," Jaime said, "what I wanted to tell you is that the house has been sealed off. I don't know when they'll let me back inside, because the sheriff's department is calling it a crime scene."

She held the phone away from her ear and still winced when Roger shouted.

"Were you hurt? A crime scene? What happened? Did someone break in? It's not as if there's anything to steal in there. Was it vandalism? Kids will do just about anything these days. You should get some security cameras."

"Not vandalism," Jaime said.

"It—ah." Roger's rant came to an abrupt halt. "Then what was it?"

She took a deep breath and told him. When she finished, he asked gently, "Are you okay? That couldn't have been easy."

"I'm . . . fine," she said. She wasn't, but she would be. Eventually. "I appreciate you asking." And she did. Roger wasn't the most presentable guy in the world, and she was sure he wasn't ever going to win any Best Attorney Ever awards, but he was a very nice man.

"What did your parents say?" Roger asked.

"Um. Well . . ." The phone vibrated in her hand. She took a quick look. "That's my mom calling now. I'd better take that."

"We'll talk tomorrow," Roger said, but as she started to tap him off and her mom on, another incoming call showed up on the screen.

She swallowed and picked up the new call.

"Detective Scoles," she said, "this is Jaime Moore. What can I do for you, sir?"

"Ms. Moore, if you have time, I'd appreciate you coming into the sheriff's office within the next hour."

"Oh. Um. Okay." She wondered if she should call Roger. "Can I ask what this is about?"

There was a short pause. Then he said, "We've identified the body in your wall."

Chapter Five

The very small room Jaime had been ushered into was occupied by four chairs, a table, and absolutely nothing else. Well, nothing else other than Jaime, Detective Scoles, and a young deputy whose name badge indicated a last name of Hoxie, but whose first name she'd already forgotten. And though the table that separated Jaime from the detective and his coworker wasn't large, it felt like a vast abyss, keeping the knowledgeable on one side, and the ignorant on the other. "That can't be right," Jaime said. "I mean, I know her."

Detective Scoles nodded. "From her age, I thought you might. In high school together, then?"

"Yes. Well, sort of. I was two years younger than Cilla." Jaime blinked and shook her head. "Cilla Price," she murmured. "I can't believe it."

"What can you tell us about Ms. Price?" Detective Scoles asked.

Jaime tried to gather her thoughts, currently whirling about in wild circles, into something that resembled coherence. "Smart, pretty, confident. Everybody knew her. She was one of those people who was going to do big things. Going to be somebody important." All the things that Jaime had never been. Sure, she'd been an important part of King Contractors, but since that was now lost to her, she couldn't count that as a success.

"Sorry," Jaime said. "That kind of stuff probably isn't what you're interested in."

The detective smiled. "Tell us anything you can remember. You never know what might be helpful."

Jaime nodded. "Okay." She thought backward to her freshman year. She'd been placed in a number of advanced classes, which resulted in self-imposed social isolation because what did she have in common with those older kids? The highlight had been when the popular football-playing, track-running, wide-smiling Henry King—a sophomore!—had asked for her help with algebra. But Cilla Price had been a junior then, and in a completely different social sphere.

"She was nice," Jaime said softly, "when she didn't have to be. Nice when no one was looking, if that makes any sense."

The deputy looked at the detective, got a nod, and asked, "Can you give us an example?"

A memory surfaced. "I had a dentist appointment and was late to school. Our dentist was downtown, nót that far from school. Only it poured rain."

The memory of the cold, wet rain made her shiver. "I came in the front door, soaked to the skin. It was during class, and there wasn't anyone around, but Cilla was on some errand and saw me walk in. She could have laughed or ignored me or said something like 'Nice weather for ducks,' and kept walking. Instead, she took one look and grabbed my elbow. Towed me into the girls' locker room, found me a towel, got me some dry socks, and"—she put a hand to her head, remembering—"she did a fast French braid on my hair. I was a nobody, but she did that for me."

"Sounds like a nice person," the deputy commented.

Shaking away the foggy past, she said, "Yes. She was. I've only run into her a couple of times since high school, but my parents know hers"—although she couldn't remember how or why—"so Mom and Dad give me updates once in a while."

"It'll take us time to gather that information," Detective Scoles said. "Telling us what you remember will be helpful."

"She went to UNC at Chapel Hill, I know that for sure." Lara had said she'd seen Cilla on the University of North Carolina campus a couple of times. "After college she moved to southern California and worked for a media company of some kind—I don't remember the name, sorry—doing human resource stuff."

"And then?" the deputy asked.

Jaime rubbed her temples. "Then a couple of years ago her grandmother died, and she came home to live with her grandfather."

Detective Scoles tipped his head in a questioning sort of way. "That's quite a life change for the sake of a grandparent."

"Like I said, I didn't know Cilla that well." Jaime shrugged, because the move had seemed weird to her too. "Maybe she just wanted to come home. Anyway, she got a job as HR manager for that new place out on River Road, that factory that makes computer chips. I think her grandfather died, maybe a year ago."

"Carolina Semiconductors," the detective said. "They're a local subsidiary of a national company."

That sounded right. Jaime nodded. "And that's all I remember. Wish I could be more help."

"We appreciate your cooperation," Detective Scoles said.

Jaime got the feeling he was about to do the go-away-and-don't-bother-us routine, so she quickly said, "Can I ask some questions?"

"Go ahead," the detective said. "Although we may not be able to answer them."

She nodded. "I get that. How did you figure out it was Cilla so quickly?"

"Almost like TV, right?" Detective Scoles smiled. "But the answer is simple. One of the first things we check is missing persons. Ms. Price was reported as such three weeks ago. The woman in your wall had an artificial knee. So did Ms. Price. She took up surfing in California, and a bad wipeout, on top of earlier soccer injuries, resulted in a knee replacement. The device's serial number was damaged and indistinct, but the medical examiner obtained Ms. Price's dental records and was able to confirm identity."

Jaime remembered that Cilla had been a star soccer player, good enough to get a college scholarship. Maybe her knee surgery was part of the reason she'd come back to Green River.

"However," the detective was saying, "it'll take some time to determine a cause of death. All I can tell you now is that the manner of death wasn't natural."

"So . . . Cilla was murdered?" Jaime asked.

"One doesn't usually," the detective said kindly, "get entombed in a wall through lawful means."

Jaime colored. How did she get to be thirty-two years old and still manage to ask such stupid questions? "I mean, do you have any idea what happened? Lara and I, we thought the body was old, and . . ."

And instead it was Cilla. Someone she'd known. Someone she'd liked.

"Under investigation," Detective Scoles said. "Sorry. As soon as we finish processing the house, we'll let you know."

He thanked her again. The deputy walked her outside, making idle small talk, but Jaime's responses were at best distracted and at worst totally inappropriate.

Because she could only think one thing.

Now she really had to talk to her mother.

*   *   *

"Why is it," her mother said, hands on her slim hips and glaring daggers, "that I have to hear what's going on with my daughter from strangers and not my own flesh and blood?"

"Hello to you too." Jaime shut the door of her truck—gently, so as not to dislodge any of the rust that was holding it together—and headed up the short walk to her childhood home. Her parents had bought the single-story brick house almost forty years ago, soon after they'd married, and very soon after her mom had learned she was carrying their first child. That child had turned out to be Allen, the oldest of her three older brothers.

Allen had been followed two years later by Caleb, who himself had been two when Evan was born. The standard two year interval had become four, which was when Jaime had come along.

Jaime often felt as if she had five parents, not two, as her three brothers felt compelled to tell her on a regular basis what she was doing wrong with her life. This unsolicited advice included, but was certainly not limited to, her early attempts at woodworking, the way she threw a ball, the music she listened to, the books she read, the TV shows she watched, the cars she liked, and the man she'd married.

As it turned out, they'd been right about Henry, but she held tight to her long-held conviction that a Mustang was better than a Camaro, and nothing any of them said was going to change her mind.

Jaime climbed the brick steps and kissed her mother's cheek. "Hope you and Dad have some time. There's a lot to tell you."

Her mom looked pointedly at her watch. "How long has it been since you found that body in the wall—ten hours? Twelve? And in all that time, you couldn't pick up the phone that's glued to your hip?"

Reflexively, Jaime tapped her pants pocket. Cell phone was safe and sound. "Did you and Dad eat?"

"Of course we did. It's seven o'clock." Her mom rolled her eyes. "But I made meatloaf and baked potatoes, and there's leftovers. Do you want a meatloaf sandwich? I'll make you one while you round up your father. He's in the basement, fixing the arm on a dining chair. If he's not doing that, let me know, because he promised."

"As if," Jaime said to herself, almost smiling as she went into the garage and opened the door that led to the basement workshop. Her mom probably knew that Jaime would never rat out her dad, but maybe hope sprang eternal that the mother–daughter bond would someday grow stronger than the father–daughter relationship.

Both of her parents were in their early sixties, but both looked ten years younger. It could have been due to a quirk of genetics or their solid marriage, or their hiking and biking habits. Whatever the reason or reasons, Jaime hoped she took after her parents, and not her aunts and uncles.

She stood on the bottom stair and looked at her dad, who was definitely not fixing a chair. He was wearing ear protection and holding a piece of wood in the bed of the miter saw. She plugged her fingers in her ears while he cut. When the saw was off, she flicked the light switch off and on, off and on.

Brad Moore turned, sliding the padded earmuffs from his ears, down around his neck, and smiled at his daughter. "Hey, Pumpkin. About time you showed up. Your mom was after you something fierce all through supper."

She made a face. "Why should today be any different?"

He laughed. "I suppose she sent you down here to fetch me. I'll be a minute; you go on up."

But Jaime didn't see any reason to do that, so she sat on the bottom step and watched, the same way she had throughout her childhood. She saw that the dining chair was off in a corner, covered with a thin layer of sawdust. "What are you working on?" she asked.

He gestured at a magazine on the workbench. "Was digging through my old *ShopNotes* magazines and saw plans for a crosscut sled. It was just calling my name, if you know what I mean."

Jaime smiled. She did indeed.

They chatted amicably about the plan as he took off his shop apron, hung it on a hook, and picked up a long brush.

45

"Let me." Standing, Jaime took the brush and swept the sawdust from his clothes with practiced swipes. "There. All dusted," she said, just like she had since she was four years old.

They climbed the stairs, and when they got inside the house, her mom nodded at the kitchen table. "Your dinner's in there. How's he coming along on fixing the chair?"

"Fine," Jaime said, sitting at the table in her normal spot. "He's making a jig; that way the chair arm will glue up square." A complete and utter fabrication, but she'd rather lie to her mom then get her dad in trouble. She dug into the meal her mom had whipped together: meatloaf sandwich, spinach salad, and piping-hot redskin potatoes. How she had done all that in less than five minutes, Jaime had no idea.

Her parents sat across from her, and thankfully her mom kept quiet until the plate was half empty.

"Jaime Evelyn," she said, "you have to tell us what happened this morning. Tell us everything, and I might forgive you before Thanksgiving."

"Stephany," her dad murmured.

"Don't 'Stephany' me," her mom snapped. "Hearing the news from Adele Trotter that you'd found a body in the wall of that house was enough to sour my mood for days."

Lara's mom was far from a stranger, but Jaime understood. Her mom had learned about the body from someone who wasn't her.

"Sorry," she said to her plate. "It's just . . . I didn't . . . didn't want to . . ." She sighed, shaking her head. "It was hard, I guess. It wasn't like it is on TV. This was someone who'd been a real person, right there in front of me. And now that I know who it . . ." She stopped. "You probably haven't heard. They've made an identification."

"Already?" her dad asked. "That was fast."

Her mom leaned forward. "Who is it? Anyone we know?"

"Yes." Jaime kept staring at her plate. "Cilla Price."

Her mom gasped. "Not that pretty Cilla. Surely that's wrong. They've made a mistake—they must have."

"Didn't sound like it. There were things that were . . . definitive."

"Cilla Price." Jaime's dad rubbed his jaw. "It's hard when one of our students dies before us."

Jaime waited for her parents to arrive at the obvious conclusion.

"But . . ." Her mom's eyes widened. "But that means poor Cilla was murdered."

"In the house you're working on," her dad said.

They exchanged a glance, then turned and focused on her.

No. She was not going to sit there and get drilled with questions for which she had no answers. She jumped up. "Thanks so much for dinner, Mom—it was great. Good seeing both of you, but I really have to get going. I'll see you, um . . . Sunday? Thanks again."

And before they could stop her, she fled.

Chapter Six

The next morning, Jaime was the first one awake. She rolled over, her sleeping bag rolling along with her, and thought about the day ahead of her. Yesterday morning, she'd been all bright-eyed and bushy-tailed, eager to get working on the house, full of anticipation and feeling, as if she were on the way back to being herself.

Now? Not so much.

She eased onto her back and stared at Lara's dingy white ceiling. Now she had nothing to do and nowhere to go. And Cilla Price was dead.

Okay, Cilla had been dead for a while, but no one had known that until Jaime had smashed open the wall. "Shades of 'The Cask of Amontillado,'" Jaime murmured. She'd read the Poe short story in middle school, and every so often it crept into her nightmares. That Cilla had ended up like Fortunato gave Jaime the creeps. At least she'd found Cilla in less than fifty years.

Then Jaime felt a twinge as she realized she was wrong. At least one person had known Cilla was dead—the person who'd killed her and walled her up inside the house.

"In my house," Jaime said out loud. Of all the houses in all the world, why that one? There must be lots of houses empty for one reason or another, so why had the murderer chosen the one house that Jaime owned?

She squirmed out of the sleeping bag, which was always way easier than fussing with the zipper. Then she started the coffee and got in the shower. When she came out of the bathroom, toweling her hair dry, Lara was sitting at the table, her face deep into a massive mug of coffee.

"Would you prefer a vat?" Jaime asked, getting her own midsize mug from the kitchen cabinet.

Lara raised her gaze. "You have one?"

"Not handy, no."

"Cruel woman." Lara returned to her caffeine consumption.

"I worry about you," Jaime said, sitting at the table. "It's not normal to have such a freakish need for coffee."

The corners of Lara's eyes creased in what Jaime assumed was a smile, though she wasn't sure because her friend's face was still buried in the mug. "Of all the people in my life," Lara said, "you're the one scolding me about being normal?"

Jaime didn't like where that was going, so she diverted. "I figured you'd stay at Tony's. How was dinner?"

"Out of clean clothes there, and dinner was fine. Tony's new work friends are Northerners. From Michigan."

"Did they use their hands to tell you where they used to live?"

"Nope. They're from the way north part, the Upper Peninsula, so the hand thing doesn't work as well. Small favors, right? They're fun, so we'll probably do something with them again. How did it go with your mom?" Lara slid her a sideways glance.

"About what you'd expect, and thanks so very little for not warning me that you'd talked to your mom. But I have to tell you something." Jaime cupped her hands around her mug. "After you left yesterday, Detective Scoles called. They've identified the . . . body we found."

"That was fast." There was a slight thud as Lara's coffee bowl landed on the table. "It was someone who'd been there for decades, right? Maybe even longer, to look all dried up like that."

When Lara rattled to a stop, Jaime said, "This happened recently. And it's someone we know." She pulled in a deep breath and told her about Cilla Price.

Lara's eyes went round. "But . . . that's . . . that can't be right."

Jaime told her about the missing persons report and the knee replacement.

"I don't understand." Lara stared at the air. "None of this makes any sense. Cilla dead? Looking like she'd spent a thousand years in the desert?" She shuddered. "And in your house? I don't get it. Why? Why do any of it?"

Jaime didn't understand either, and they weren't any closer to understanding when the coffee was gone, breakfast was eaten, and Lara had to leave for work. At the front door, briefcase in hand, she said, "You'll keep me updated as you work through the spreadsheet, right? And you need to push Bax Scoles on getting back into the house. They can't keep you out forever."

Though Lara was probably right, Jaime wasn't sure that pestering the detective would speed up the process.

She washed the coffee mugs and the cereal bowls and thought about her day. Next on Lara's spreadsheet, aka The List, was talking to Henry and to Bob McNinch. And she should probably talk to Roger again, now that Cilla had been identified.

That had to wait, though, at least for a few hours. What she needed to do first was talk to her subcontractors. Her electrician. Her plumber. Roofer. Drywaller. Painter. All of them. The way word had spread about the body, they might have already heard, but she'd learned early on in the contracting business that bad news delivered with an apologetic smile and a heartfelt sigh tended to go down easier.

She flipped open her own laptop and scrolled through the project spreadsheet, reading the notes she'd made about her subs. Most of them were working close by; she should be able to talk to most of them that morning.

Fifteen minutes later, she pulled into a downtown parking lot, parked next to a truck with "Riverside Electricians" painted on the doors, and crossed the lot, heading straight toward the drilling noise.

Her friend Glory Aprelle had taken over Riverside from her father a few years ago, and business, after a few bumps, had never been better. As it turned out, there were a lot of women who needed electrical work, and the vast majority of them were more than pleased to hire a woman.

Jaime pushed aside the sheets of plastic that were the current door to the former insurance agency and stepped inside. Glory was on a tall stepladder, her head and shoulders hidden inside a dropped ceiling.

She peered upward. "Hey, Ms. Master Electrician! You have a minute?"

"Be there in a sec," Glory's muffled voice said. "There's coffee if you want."

She did not, so she wandered to the front window and looked out at the street, empty except for three men about her age, dressed in black jeans and black T-shirts, carrying expensive-looking cameras and lighting equipment. "What's going on out there?" she asked as her friend descended the ladder and brushed the dust out of her short-cropped hair.

"No idea," Glory said. "They've been out there since dawn. Something for the Chamber of Commerce, I guess. What's up?"

Jaime had rehearsed a speech, as she knew she'd have to deliver it over and over that day. She put her hands in the pockets of her spring coat. "It's about my house . . ."

When Jaime was done, Glory was still shaking her head. "She was a couple years younger than me, but I remember her. No one deserves to be walled up like that, let alone Cilla. She was the nicest girl. Always did the right thing, you know? She should have passed to the other side when she was old, in her sleep, after a life of good work. Like that? It's just plain wrong."

"Yes," Jaime said. "It certainly is."

Right then and there, she vowed to make things right. Nothing would bring Cilla back, but if she could help right a wrong, she would. For the sake of justice, sure, but mostly to help Cilla, wherever she was, rest more easily.

* * *

Jaime hunted down one subcontractor after another, and by the end of the morning, she'd talked to all of them. Not all were as understanding as Glory had been, which wasn't a huge surprise given how busy everyone was, but waiting was the only thing to do.

"How long a delay are we talking about?" asked Frank Gribbon, her plumber, whose salt and pepper hair, fitness, and sentence structure were more Wall Street than crawl spaces and under-the-kitchen-sink-type spaces. He wasn't from Green River, and how he'd ended up there, Jaime had no idea, but she was happy that he had. He was an excellent plumber, and since he hadn't known her from childhood, he didn't pat her on the head and tell her she'd grown up into a pretty little lady.

Jaime shook her head, shrugging. "Sorry, Frank. There's no way to tell. Might be two days, might be two weeks."

"Might it be two months?"

"Two months?" she echoed, and tried to calm her brain, which was suddenly freaking out. It couldn't take that long—it just couldn't, because that would mess up everything. Two months from now, most of her subcontractors were scheduled to be working on the big battery plant going in halfway between Green River and Charlotte. They wouldn't have time to get back to her project until late fall, which meant she'd have to find other subcontractors, and these were the subs she wanted. The subs that she trusted. And maybe most importantly, there were the subs willing to take her carpentry in trade. If she couldn't keep these subs on her job, the numbers wouldn't work. It would be all over.

She stuck a smile on her face. "I'm sure it won't take that long," she told Frank. "I'll be in contact with the sheriff's office once a day—no, *twice* a day—until they release the house."

"You've never seemed like someone who subscribes to the Squeaky Wheel Theory," he said, considering her.

"I've never had to." And it was true. She believed in working hard, in treating everyone with respect, and in not complaining, because things could always be worse.

Now? Now, maybe not so much. She'd worked hard for fifteen years at her marriage and at King Contractors, and what had it gotten her? Cilla, from what Jaime knew, had also worked hard and she'd been . . . she'd been . . .

Jaime tried to swallow the lump suddenly stuck in her throat. She'd known people who'd died. Her grandparents. The dad of one of her friends. But this was different. This was someone her age. Someone who shouldn't be dead. Someone who'd had her life stolen from her. And that made everything so very much worse.

It was lunchtime and Jaime was fairly sure the morning had lasted fifteen years, so even though her entertainment budget was tight, she decided to treat herself to another lunch out. "After this," she told herself, "you have to stick to the plan."

Although what her plan was, exactly, she couldn't be sure, because none of the scenarios she'd developed over the last couple of months had included anything close to what had happened yesterday morning.

She made a mental note to call Detective Scoles later on in the day to start her first-ever Squeaky Wheel Campaign, then thought about a lunch place. Frank had been working at a house outside of town, miles from any restaurants, but not too far from the industrial park, which meant the odds of finding a food truck or two were good, especially on such a nice spring morning.

At the entrance to the industrial park, two food trucks had set up shop. One was selling burgers and fries; the other was one of Jaime's favorite trucks in the area, Terry's Tacos. She pulled onto the grassy shoulder, and ten minutes later was sitting cross-legged on the opened tailgate of her truck, happily eating her triple taco selection: one chicken, one fish, and one shrimp.

She inhaled the fish taco and was trying to decide which one should come next, when she heard heavy footsteps. She looked up and saw Roger, his hair mussed, tie loose, and shirt buttoned one button off.

"Jaime?" her attorney frowned. "What are you doing out here?"

She was not about to tell her attorney and a man who was one of her dad's best friends that she'd been groveling in front of her subcontractors in the hopes that they wouldn't bail on her project. "Eating. How about you?"

"Me? Well, I was out here to talk to, ah, one of my clients. And now it's lunchtime." He chuckled jovially. "Taco or burger, that is the question. I see you chose tacos."

"Terry's are the best," she said. "Roger, I need to tell you something else. About yesterday."

"Please don't tell me you found a second body."

Jaime squinted at him. Had that been a joke? Sometimes it was hard to tell with Roger. "They made an identification."

"That was fast. I thought the timelines they show on TV were a fantasy."

"In most cases, they probably are." Jaime put the shrimp taco down and picked up the chicken. Saving the best for last. "In this case, though, the body matched a missing persons report, and there was a—what do you call it?—a confirming characteristic."

"Oh?" Roger looked past her. "Sounds unusual."

She could tell he was far more interested in his lunch than in her story, so she zipped to the end. "It was someone I went to high school with. Not sure you knew her, but it was Cilla Price."

"What?"

His attention snapped straight to her, drilling her with a sharpened gaze she'd never seen from this easygoing man, and she got the sudden feeling that Roger walked through most of his days slightly asleep.

"Cilla Price," Jaime said again. "She was two years older than me. Really nice person. She'd moved to California after college, but came back a few—"

"Yes," he interrupted sharply. "I know the name. She's . . . oh, goodness. This is . . . oh, my goodness. I have to . . . yes, I have to go." He hurried back down the road's shoulder, back to where he'd parked his car.

Jaime started to get up, then sat back down. A flustered Roger was even harder to talk to than a regular Roger, and flustered he certainly was. But . . . why?

She frowned at her tacos, not liking where her thoughts were going.

Because she'd realized one very obvious thing: Roger had held a key to the house.

For weeks.

Chapter Seven

With her stomach in that sweet spot of full, but not too full, Jaime decided it was time to tackle the last thing in the world she wanted to do: talk to Henry. If she didn't do it soon, Lara would start hounding her, and then she'd get irritated about the hounding and put it off even longer.

"Just get it over with," Jaime muttered.

She was not—absolutely not—keeping track of the projects King Contractors was working on these days, but because of typical construction timelines, she'd been the one to sign the contracts for most of their current projects, and she'd set up the work schedules.

In time, she assumed all that knowledge would erase itself from her head, or at least fade enough that she couldn't recall details, but part of the problem was so many project sites were local. There was one she couldn't possibly avoid, as it was just a mile up the road from her parents' house. The Andersons' house was an old bungalow that had been rented out for decades, and she'd spent hours and hours with them, working out how best to bring the place into twenty-first-century living.

Jaime parked at the curb and hoped that someone had figured out how to locate the Anderson's attic skylight. They were both artists, and getting it in just the right location had been way high on their priority list.

She sat in her truck, staring at her hands on the steering wheel, planning what she was going to say to Henry, when there a whack on the hood.

"Hey, girl!" A fiftyish Black man was staring at her, leaning forward, his hands flat on the metal. Then he grinned. "Get out here and give an old man a hug."

Jaime slid from the driver's seat and into the big arms of Bob McNinch, the King Contractors foreman. She hadn't seen him since . . . well, since That Day, and she was glad to finally know, for sure, that he still liked her. Maybe even cared about her.

"You've lost weight," he said, releasing her and giving her a quick once-over. "Looks like I need to bake my world-famous coconut cream pie and watch you eat every single bite."

"And you've put on weight." She poked him in the belly with her forefinger. "Looks like you need some exercise."

"Don't you go sounding like my doctor," he said, frowning. "Or my wife. I already have one of each."

She smiled. "As long as you don't sound like my mom or dad."

"Fair enough, fair enough," he said, laughing. "So tell me, what can I do you for?" Bob adjusted his Duke University baseball hat, hooked his thumbs in his belt loops, and shifted into an easy slouch. Just like old times. "If you're looking for your ex, he's in the backyard, siting the outdoor kitchen."

"Thanks. I need to talk to him about the house. The one I own."

Bob slid a glance Henry-ward. "Yeah, sorry about that place. I should have tried harder to get it sold."

Though Jaime appreciated the thought, if the house had been sold pre-divorce, she would have ended up with even less than she had now. Sure, she couldn't get inside, and the forensic people were surely making an even bigger mess of it, adding who knew what cost to a project with delays that could bankrupt her, but at least it was a house. A project. There was nothing she liked better than a big project, and if Henry thought that by leaving her that wreck of a house he was in some way punishing her, well, then he'd never really known her at all.

Then Jaime realized that Bob wasn't talking about what she'd assumed he'd be talking about. "You haven't heard what happened out there yesterday morning?"

Bob tipped his head back and closed his eyes halfway. "Heard what?"

Jaime told the story of smashing the wall to smithereens, finding a body, calling the police, being kicked out of the house, and then learning whose body she'd found.

"Whoa. That's quite a thing." Bob stared at the sky. "So she was murdered. Had to be, right?"

""Yeah." And here was the big question. "Was the house easy to get into? Like, a key under the flowerpot? Something everyone knew about?"

"Don't think so," Bob said, shaking his head. "But I was only in there once. You'll have to ask Henry."

"Ask me what?"

Jaime's neck went rigid with tension. She turned her head. He was still six feet tall, still had hair that needed a cut, still had broad shoulders and a square face that looked as if belonged in a movie set in the Wild West. He wasn't any different, but she was. She no longer cared what he thought about her.

"Hello, Henry," she said pleasantly. Or as pleasantly as she could through gritted teeth. Though she was beyond pleased that her primary reaction to this first post-divorce meeting was irritation, she would have been even more pleased to have put off the meeting even longer. Months. Years, even.

"Oh. It's you," he said flatly. "What are you doing here?"

Bob inched away. "Um . . ."

"That house on Holt Road." She put her chin up and glared at the man she'd been in love with for so many years. Had she really been stupid enough to fall for his good looks without ever noticing his shallow personality? The answer was, obviously, yes—but really? "In the time King Contractors owned it, who had possession of the keys?"

"I held the set in the office the whole time." He smirked. "Why? Did you lose them?"

His shallow and petty personality. "The police want to know," she said.

"Police?" The smirk rearranged itself into a sneer. "Didn't I say? You'll never make it without me. Can't believe you've managed to screw up the house I gave you this fast. Must be a new record."

His shallow, petty, and vindictive personality. Opting not to erupt over the "I gave you" bit, she snapped out, "Sorry. I thought you'd want to know that the house is a murder scene. Victim is Cilla Price. Yes, that Cilla, the one we went to high school with, remember?"

But Henry was shaking his head. "Nope. I really don't."

"Doesn't matter." She shrugged. "Even if it had been King Tut, the police would still want to talk to you. But with Cilla, I bet it's only a matter of time before the police show up, thinking you're a murder suspect."

She spun around, jumped into her driver's seat, and was away before Henry had gathered his wits enough to respond.

As she drove, she took deep breaths, let her fast-beating heart slow, and forced herself to think.

Henry had held the house key.

Just like Roger.

But also like Roger, why would Henry have murdered Cilla?

*   *   *

59

She got a large dose of satisfaction when she looked in the rearview mirror and saw Henry staring at her truck, mouth wide open, but two miles down the road, she realized she had no idea where she was going. Or what she was doing. Or even what she should be doing.

She'd spent a lot of weeks, too many of them, slouching on Lara's couch, binge-watching more TV shows than she could count, and she'd only recently pulled herself out of the funk she'd fallen into. The funk that she'd *let* herself fall into, she reminded herself. Henry had been a cheating you-know-what, and he and his father had cheated her out of what should have been hers, but she shouldn't have let that take her over. She shouldn't have let it consume her or let it drive her life for so long.

"Never again," she said out loud. From now on, it would be different. Her life would never circle around a man so tightly. She would have a focus, a mission, goals, and principles to guide her that didn't involve anyone other than herself. What her focused mission with guiding principles and goals might be, exactly, she didn't know, but that was something she could start working on. Soon. Maybe even that day.

A phrase floated into her thoughts: Reasons or results? If she recalled correctly, Lara had read it to her from some book, and the words had snuck into her long-term memory. Which matters more: having a ton of reasons for not reaching your objective; or doing the work, no matter what, and actually achieving what you'd set out to do?

What she needed, though, was a better understanding of the results she wanted in her life. What she needed was a set of goals. As Jaime drove slowly into Green River's downtown, she realized that she did have one goal. Maybe she didn't have her life goals mapped out, but she did have that house.

It had been the lure of a rewarding house project that had pulled her off Lara's couch and propelled her back into the world. The thought of people in those rooms, laughing, cooking, and celebrating holidays filled her with a sense of happiness that had no comparison.

She pulled into a parking space in the lot behind the hardware store. Changing her life trajectory wouldn't really be that simple, because beyond renovating this house, she wasn't completely sure what shape she wanted the rest of her life to take. But this house was a start—a focused start—and that was enough to go on.

Whistling, she walked in through the back door. She'd been coming to Gardner's with her dad since before she could talk, and one deep breath of the complex mix of smells that made up Gardner's Hardware Store comforted her like nothing else could. If Jaime had been led there blindfolded, she would have known where she was within half a second. Nowhere else in the world could smell like Gardner's: a little machine oil and a little paint, along with a bit of male sweat and cigar smoke, all embedded into the wood floor over a period of decades.

"Hey, Ms. Jaime."

"Randy." She nodded at the sixtyish man who was stocking the sandpaper. "Did your wife's surgery go okay?" A week earlier, Randy Johnston's wife—whose first name, as far she knew, was Momma—had tripped over their dog's leash. She'd fallen hard on the sidewalk, hitting shoulder first.

"Yeah, thanks for asking." He lined up the boxes of eighty-grit sandpaper precisely. "Four weeks in a cast, then physical therapy, but Momma should be a hundred percent by football season." He grinned. "Pretty sure our oldest grandson's going to be on the starting line."

"They can train together," Jaime suggested.

Randy laughed. "That's a fine picture. Can't wait to tell Momma. That will tickle her funny bone something fierce. Now, what can I do for you today?"

"Need a new sledge. A twelve-pounder."

"You just bought one of those. Did it break? Because you know we have a lifetime guarantee for hand tools."

"No, no." She shook her head. "It's fine." But there was no way she was going to be able to use it again. She wasn't superstitious, it was just that . . . okay, maybe she was superstitious. "I just need another one, is all. Do you have any that have a handle color other than orange?"

"Hmm." Randy rubbed his chin. "Not sure about that one, but maybe Mike knows. He's picking up some different suppliers. Say, have you met the new manager? He's been here, what, four months now?"

"Almost six."

The voice sounded vaguely familiar. Jaime turned and was face to face with Mike Darden, another nonowner of the cat that wasn't hers. So that was why she'd thought she'd seen him somewhere before. Though she hadn't spent much time in Gardner's since the day she'd found living, breathing poof of Henry's infidelity, at some point Mike's presence must have registered.

Likely she'd unconsciously avoided him in a self-protective way, as the physical resemblance between Mike and Henry was a real thing. Six feet in height, dark hair, wide swimmer's shoulders, square faces, strong jaws. If some movie director had wanted to cast for tall, dark, and handsome, they would both have filled the qualifications easily.

But now that she was getting a second, closer look at Mike Darden, she was sensing some basic differences. Both men projected confidence, but Henry had always done so with an in-your-face kind of way, while Mike was coming across as self-assured. Comfortable in his own skin. Happy with himself and where he was. It was, Jaime realized, a very attractive trait, and she found herself smiling at him.

"Hi," she said. "I didn't realize you worked here."

"And I didn't realize you were Jaime Moore, one of the three women in Green River to carry an account with Gardner's Hardware."

"Glory Aprelle," she said promptly. "And Violet Dilworth."

Mike laughed, revealing front teeth with the tiniest gap, something that Henry did not have. Jaime was happy to see a difference between the two men and also decided not to explore the origin behind that happiness.

"So you're from here, I take it," he said.

"Born and bred."

After that, the conversation lagged.

Randy went on stocking sandpaper. Jaime watched him and approved of the way he squared up the corners of all the boxes.

"So," she said, eventually. "Sledgehammers."

"Right." Mike nodded. "You bet. A twelve, you say?"

"Ideally, with a yellow handle."

"Let's go take a look."

He moved off, and though Jaime wouldn't have sworn to it, she was pretty sure she heard Randy say, "He'll treat you better than Henry did."

After a long search, Mike found a sledge that met every one of Jaime's qualifications, which was really only one: that it not be anything like the one she'd used to knock down the wall that had sealed in Cilla Price.

He pulled an honest-to-goodness handkerchief from the back pocket of his pants and dusted it off before handing it to her. "Sorry about that. I'm still working on organizing stock."

"No worries," she said. "It's a sledgehammer. They're supposed to get dirty."

"Good point." He waved her forward, to take the lead in the trek back upstairs and through the shelving maze.

Figuring there was a close to one hundred percent chance that he was watching her climb the stairs, Jaime was too self-conscious to think of a thing to say the entire walk to the front register, so instead of sounding stupid, she chose not to say anything, and ended up feeling like an introverted contractor. Which was what she was, so she was okay with that.

"On your account?" Mike asked as he went around behind the counter. At her nod, he said, "Sounds good. Need a receipt?"

She shook her head.

"Good by me," he said cheerfully. "I'm working on moving our point of sales fully electronic. Going to take some doing, but we'll get there eventually."

Jaime thought the former manager, who'd run Gardner's for about a hundred years, must be rolling over in his grave, but she agreed wholeheartedly with the concept. Most of the contractors would too, although there would be holdouts, and not necessarily the older ones. Henry for sure wouldn't like it. He preferred cash whenever possible.

She frowned. What was she doing, thinking about Henry?

"Thanks," she muttered, then took her new sledgehammer and headed to the back door. She had her hand on the push bar when she saw Randy. She paused. "Did you say something?"

He looked toward the front, where Mike was still at the register, then turned back to Jaime and smiled, his face creasing into deep lines. "Just to have a nice day."

"You too," she said, and opened the door so fast she almost hit the outside wall. The last thing she needed was Randy Johnston playing matchmaker. Sure, she'd known him since before she could walk, but she'd known lots of people that long, and that didn't give any of them the right to interfere in her life.

"Not anyone." She opened the lid of her truck's bed cover and tossed the sledge inside. Not Randy, not Lara, not her parents. She shut the lid with a bang. "Not anymore."

"I'm sorry, I didn't catch what you said?" A pretty young woman standing by the bright yellow convertible parked next door smiled at her over the lumpy shopping bags she was trying to stuff into her car's trunk. "You don't have anyone? Was that it?"

Natalie Blake. Even in Jaime's head, she said the name with a curled lip. She kept hoping she'd forget what she'd seen last fall, but she couldn't seem to erase the memory of finding Natalie and Henry, both of them as naked as the day they were born, wrapped up together. Worse, she had found them in the house Jaime had been lovingly restoring as the house she and Henry would live in the rest of their lives.

"You poor thing," Natalie said, shutting the trunk and panting a little at the effort . "All alone in life. If you'd taken better care of your man, maybe he wouldn't have strayed."

Jaime reverted to her mother's instruction—*If you don't have anything nice to say, don't say anything*"—and opened the door of her truck. Besides, witty comebacks were not her strength, so engaging with Natalie was a no-win situation. Her best strategy was to ignore the woman.

"And now you have to deal with a murder in your very own house," Natalie said, sighing. "You poor thing. And that poor—what was her name? Oh yes. Cilla Price. Whatever did she do to end up like that, all dried up and sealed inside a wall?"

Jaime shut her truck door, but since she'd left the windows down, she kept on hearing the piercing voice.

"It was nice talking to you, Jaime King . . . oh, dear, that's not right, is it?" Natalie giggled. "You're back to where you started, You're just plain old Jaime Moore now, aren't you?"

The truck's engine revved as Jaime's right work boot pressed on the accelerator. In her side mirror, she saw Natalie's high-heeled strappy red sandals scurry off, and smiled at the sight.

She knew the anger she felt toward Natalie mostly belonged on Henry's shoulders, and that she should be working to forgiveness. Or something. But it was hard to forgive, let alone forget, when That Woman had moved in with Henry a handful of weeks after That Day.

"Not even a month," Jaime said, pounding the steering wheel. "How could I have been so stupid?"

For that was what she kept coming back to. How could she not have seen the signs? How could she have been so blind? Henry had been the one to insist that King Contractors needed to hire an office receptionist, saying that Jaime was working too hard, that she needed help even though Jaime had never once felt overworked. Next thing she knew, he'd hired Natalie. She'd always thought spouses being cheated on must have some idea, deep down, that something was going on, but she really and truly hadn't.

And there she was, thinking about Henry again. She did not want to think about him. Or Natalie. But . . . she thought back to her conversation with Henry. He'd said he didn't remember Cilla Price, which was ridiculous. There was no way he could have forgotten Cilla. Their high school graduated little more than a hundred students a year; everybody knew everybody in their class and in the classes a year above and below.

Either Henry was a clueless and oblivious idiot, or he was lying. Either option was possible. Actually, both options were simultaneously possible. This amused her, and she snorted a short laugh.

Then there was Natalie. Natalie, with the perfect smile, the perfect hair, and the perfect body, was one of those shiny people who tended to intimidate Jaime, not that she'd admit that to anyone.

But maybe Natalie had issues of her own. Why had she gone to the trouble of being so nasty to Jaime when she could have simply walked past her? Was Natalie insecure about her own relationship with Henry? Did Jaime's presence threaten her?

And what was it she'd said about Cilla: *"Whatever did she do to end up like that, all dried up and sealed inside a wall?"* How did Natalie know so many details? Yes, it was a small town and news traveled fast, but that was a lot of information.

Maybe Natalie knew Cilla. Maybe they'd had an argument. Maybe Natalie had murdered Cilla in a fit of rage, because she clearly had anger management issues. And maybe she'd sealed Cilla's body in that house because she saw it as the perfect way to ruin Jaime's life a second time.

The more Jaime thought about it, the more she liked it.

Now all she had to do was find some proof.

Chapter Eight

Jaime found a quiet, shady side street and pulled to the curb. Cilla had been in the Human Resources Department at Carolina Semiconductor. CS, as most people called it, had done a huge expansion a while back, which coincided with the hiring of a full time HR director. If Jaime remembered correctly . . . she tapped at her phone, opening up Facebook to check . . . Yes! She tapped some more, then held the phone to her ear.

"Jaime!" said the cheerful voice on the other end.

Ann Marie Dawkins was a fortyish software engineer, another woman in a traditionally man's world. A few years ago, she'd come to King Contractors with the dream to renovate the house where her grandmother had been born. The house was a neglected, water-damaged, termite-infested mess, and basically had been for the thirty years since Ann Marie's parents had sold and moved away, but Jaime had seen the longing in her face and found a way to make it work.

Thanks to social media, Jaime knew that Ann Marie had since married a man from Charleston, was interested in hiking the Appalachian Trail, had a passion for finding the best diner biscuits on the face of the earth—and that she worked for CS.

"Heard about you and Henry," Ann Marie said. "About time you got rid of that guy. He was holding you back. Good for you."

"Oh, um . . ." Jaime heard the questioning tone of her voice and hated herself for it. "Thanks," she said more firmly. "How are things with you? How's the house?"

"House is great. My husband—someday you'll have to meet him—thinks the upstairs shower design you came up with should win awards." Ann Marie laughed. "So, all in all, things are good, except . . . well, there's some stuff going on at work."

"Cilla Price," Jamie said.

There was a short silence. "How," Ann Marie said slowly, "do you know about that? It hasn't hit the paper yet."

"That's what I wanted to talk to you about." Jaime looked at the clock on her dashboard. Midafternoon. "Would you have a few minutes for me if I swing by? I'll bring you a bag of Tracy's cookies," she said in a wheedling tone.

Ann Marie groaned. "You know my weaknesses, don't you? See you in half an hour."

Twenty-nine minutes later, Jaime slid into a visitors space in the vast parking lot of the semiconductor manufacturing facility. She hopped out of her truck and grabbed the white paper bag of half a dozen cookies from the Chestnut Street Bakery, owned and run by Tracy Linka.

"Over here!" Ann Marie waved to her from a bench tucked into a small grove of trees near the building's entrance. "I brought the coffee."

Jaime smiled. During the long renovation process, she and Ann Marie had fallen into a serious cookies-and-coffee rut that apparently they were never going to bounce out of, something that didn't bother her in the least.

"Chocolate chip and walnut," she said, sitting and handing Ann Marie the bag. "They were all out of the white chocolate and macadamia nut."

Ann Marie took one. "It was always a tie between the two. This saves me the energy of having to make a choice, so thanks."

It was that laid-back attitude that had made Ann Marie one of her favorite clients. "So," she said, reaching for the offered coffee. "Cilla Price."

"Yeah." Ann Marie slumped. "We're reeling. She was scheduled to take a vacation, out to California to visit friends, I think it was. But then she . . . never came back. And now we hear she's dead, found sealed up in a wall like some Egyptian mummy." She shook her head. "That's the story going around, anyway. No idea how accurate it is."

"It's actually pretty close." Jaime studied the top of her coffee cup. "I was the one who found her."

"What?" Ann Marie's eyelids widened. "How?"

Jaime told her the whole story, ending with, "It's awful. I knew Cilla in high school, and she was great."

"She was." Ann Marie nodded. "Smart. Funny. Easy to work with. She knew her stuff, and I'm not just talking about human resource stuff. She was curious about all sorts of things, liked to know how things worked. She said learning about the chip design and build process helped her understand the employees better, which helped her do her job better."

Jaime thought back to her drowned-rat day in high school. Cilla had instantly understood her situation and then done something about it. HR was the perfect career for her. "We were Facebook friends," Jaime said, "but that's about it."

"I miss her. A lot. We all do. And it's hard, knowing she was murdered, dead for days and none of us knew about it, we were just going on with our lives."

The door behind them opened, and a tall, stocky man with graying hair strode past. "Ann Marie," he said, nodding. "Nice day for an outside coffee break, I take it?"

"Warren," Ann Marie said, bobbing her head slightly. "It certainly is."

Not pausing in his walk, he slid his gaze over Jaime and headed to a black Ford Expedition in a nearby parking space. He chirped the driver's door open and was driving out of the lot seconds later.

Jaime peered at the small sign marking the now-vacant parking spot. "Chief Operating Officer?"

"Mmm." Ann Marie took another cookie. "Warren Brookshire. The boss."

"Doesn't sound like you're a fan."

She shrugged. "Typical upper management. He sets unrealistic goals we're supposed to meet, and then when we fail, he uses that as an excuse not to give us raises."

Once again, Jaime was reminded of why she liked working for herself so much. "Sounds brutal."

"Normal corporate game playing. Happens all over the place, all the time." Ann Marie shrugged again and looked in the direction that Brookshire had gone. "Tell you what, though," she said. "Warren is probably the one person at CS who isn't sad that Cilla's gone. The two of them had run-ins all the time. He said she lacked the ability to compromise. She said there was no compromising on the need to comply with state and federal laws."

"More normal corporate game playing?" Jaime's work experience began and ended with King Contractors, so she had no idea what was typical in big companies.

Ann Marie half smiled. "Happens in every place I've ever worked," she said wryly, "so I'm going to say yes."

Jaime took another cookie and filed the information in the back corner of her head.

* * *

It was late afternoon when Jaime drove back to Green River. She turned the radio volume up to distract her thoughts from spiraling around the idea that she hadn't accomplished a single thing on the house that day, but turned it off when the third song in a row featured a cheating partner.

"Really?" she asked out loud as she stabbed the button. As if she didn't have enough to depress her, now even the radio was testing her newfound resolve to get her life back on track. "You couldn't play something happier? Beach Boys, maybe?"

One of these days she'd have to figure out what type of connector she needed to hook her newish phone to her old truck so she could play downloaded songs. That kind of thing had been Henry's job. Of course, she'd been asking him for three years, and he'd never managed to find the time.

That was one more thing to add to the heap of evidence that Ann Marie, Randy, Lara, and her brothers knew what they were talking about when it came to Henry. He hadn't treated her right, hadn't for years—maybe not ever. And she'd been so stupid in love that she'd been willing to accept it.

"Not any longer," she said as she passed the Green River city limit sign.

Hearing the words out loud made her feel better. More like her old self.

"No," she murmured. She wouldn't go back to being like she used to be. She would never again be a doormat, would never again let people wipe their metaphorical feet on her. She was a person of worth and would not let herself be bullied ever again. Because when you came down to it, wasn't that what Henry had done to her for years? Bullied her? Belittled her? Cut her down on a daily basis? Destroyed her belief in her own capabilities?

"Never again," she said firmly. Saying the words out loud felt so good that she repeated them. She smiled. Maybe she *had* accomplished something that day.

She drove downtown and parked in the lot next to the county law enforcement center. As she walked to the front door, she noticed a white panel van parked in the front corner, close to the street. Its back doors were open, revealing metal racks filled with equipment that looked like it belonged on a TV news set.

Then she remembered the crew from that morning, the three guys, dressed in black, with the cameras and lights. What was it Glory had said about them—that they were doing something for the Chamber of Commerce?

It was a good day for filming, Jaime supposed, not that she knew anything about the process. But the town was looking nice. The trees were fully green, flowers were blooming, and the sun had been shining all day, so how could it not be a good day?

The guys in black were standing next to the van's front, coiling up cables and chatting amiably. She headed in their direction. "Hi," she called as she approached. "You've probably had this question a lot, but—"

She stopped. It wasn't three guys standing there talking; it was four. And the fourth wasn't a guy in black—it was Henry.

What was it with him? For months she'd successfully avoided running into him or Natalie. Why was she now seeing one of them every time she turned around?

Henry gave her a startled look that quickly transformed into a narrowed gaze. "Jaime. What do you want now?"

She spun around and walked away; head held high. She didn't want anything from him. Not then, not ever.

The murmur of male voices behind her straightened her spine and made her walk even taller.

Let him mock her. Let him joke with strangers at her expense. He had no power to hurt her—not anymore. That ship had sailed months ago, had disappeared over the horizon, and was on the other side of the world with no possibility of a return voyage.

She pushed in through the front door of the sheriff's office and entered the vestibule. For a few seconds, she closed her eyes; then she pulled in a deep breath and went inside.

"Hi, can I help you?" A dark-haired young woman looked at her through the thick glass separating the administrative offices from the main lobby.

She'd had talked through a perforated metal disc, so Jaime leaned in its direction. "I'm hoping to talk to Detective Scoles for a few minutes. Is he here? My name is Jaime Moore. I was in yesterday. About Cilla Price."

"Right. Sure. Let me call back and see if he's in." She moved to a phone and was soon nodding. When she put down the phone, she waved at the interior door Jaime had entered the day before and gestured for Jaime to come in.

The young woman pointed down a long hallway. "Fourth office on the right."

Jaime thanked her and followed the directions. The detective's workspace was bigger and tidier than she'd expected. She knocked on the doorframe and waited for Detective Scoles to wave her in.

"Have a seat, Ms. Moore. To what do I owe the pleasure?" He leaned back in his chair. "Don't tell me you've found another body."

Her throat tightened. "No." The small word came out so low it was almost a growl.

"Too soon, isn't it?" the detective said. "Sorry about that. My mama always said my sense of humor would land me in serious trouble someday."

Jaime tried to imagine the large man as a small boy and failed completely. "It's about the house," she said. "When I was here yesterday, I'm not sure I mentioned how much I need to get back in there."

"You did." The detective steepled his fingers. "And I understand your problem. Unfortunately, the crime scene folks haven't finished up. And before you ask," he said as she opened her mouth, "I can't give you a date when they will be done in there. I'm sorry."

To Jaime, it felt like the floor was crumbling away underneath her feet. If it didn't stop, she'd soon start falling and falling and never stop. She shook her head. No. There had to be a way to fix this. "Would it help speed up the investigation if I told you who had access to the house?"

The detective held up his index finger. "Your ex-husband." Up went another finger. "Your attorney." Up went a third finger. "The crew foreman for King Contractors. Did I miss anyone?"

Jaime deflated. The detective clearly knew what he was doing. In spite of Lara's spreadsheet, maybe it was pointless for her to ask around about Cilla.

"So, you don't have any idea when the forensics people will be done?" she asked, just to be sure she'd heard correctly.

"That's right." He stood. "I have your phone number, Ms. Moore. Believe me, as soon as I hear a date, or even a hint of a date when you can get back inside, I'll contact you."

"Thanks." She shook his hand and headed outside, walking fast.

Because she knew exactly what she was going to do next.

*　*　*

It was past five o'clock when Jaime pulled into the driveway. The empty driveway, she was very pleased to see. Because while she was ready, willing, and able to quote exactly what Detective Scoles had told her, she wasn't a hundred percent sure the crime scene people would agree with her interpretation.

She was going to hang her hat on the detective's statement of "when you can get back inside" meant that she could do outside work any time she wanted, including then and there. She also didn't need to rile up anyone unnecessarily, which was why she'd waited until after quitting time.

If she got in trouble with the detective tomorrow morning for doing work tonight—well, then she'd get in trouble. But tonight she was going to work. Her hands were starting to itch with the need to do something. If she didn't get some work done, if she didn't make something happen, she felt as if she might explode into a hundred thousand pieces.

She eyed the crime scene tape blocking off the porch. The tape was tied from one porch post to another, leaving the front steps themselves open to her. But she should probably work on something less obvious. No sense in getting into more trouble than she had to, right?

Jaime nodded to herself and got out of her pickup. It was ten minutes past five; there were three hours of daylight. Three and a half if she wasn't doing anything detailed. All she had to do was figure out what she could do while it was still a crime scene. But first things first.

She went to the shed, opened the door, and peered inside. Yep, there was a big dent in the food and the water was down an inch. She went back to her truck, returning with the cat food bag and water jug. After refills, she looked around. "Kitty?" she called tentatively. "Kitty, kitty?"

Nothing.

Shrugging off a vague feeling of disappointment, she replaced the cat supplies in the back of her truck, slipped on her working baseball cap, and studied her tools.

There wasn't anything she could do with the circular saw. Same with the reciprocating saw, demolition hammer, and her adorable little oscillating tool. If nothing else, she could do yard work with the rake and shovel she'd seen in the shed, but tidying yards was what you did at the end of projects, not the beginning.

Really and truly, she only had one option.

She grabbed her work gloves, tool belt, and brand-new sledgehammer, grinning like crazy on the inside. It was time to start swinging.

Even wearing work boots, there was a spring in her step as she walked to the back of the property, and she found herself whistling a Disney song, the one Snow White and the birds whistled when she was cleaning up the dwarfs' mess. Jaime wondered briefly if her project was going to have a theme song. Every renovation King Contractors ever worked had ended up with a theme song, and it had come about completely by accident.

On that very first job, Coldplay's "Viva la Vida" had played regularly on the radios the crews had put out. Hearing the song multiple times a day for months had turned into a kind of joke, and at the end of that first King Contractors job, she'd bought an MP3 file of the song and sent it to the happy homeowners, telling them the story. They'd been so tickled at the idea of their house having a theme song that they'd posted it all over social media.

Next thing Jaime knew, the owners of the next project were asking for their theme song, and a tradition was born. Most of the songs had little or nothing to do with the actual project, and everything to do with who was working the job, but it didn't seem to matter.

Jaime was, truth be told, happy to leave the tradition behind. It had ended up being a far bigger deal than it needed to be as the "Reveal" had turned into an event that had sucked up time and energy she'd far rather have spent doing something productive.

Like demolition.

She walked around the back of the shed she'd started to think of as the cat's and approached her target. It was a small and decrepit chicken coop that had long outlived its usefulness. The interior contained nothing but scraps of ancient straw. The roof had more holes than shingle, and the siding was a patchwork of plywood from numerous eras.

"Perfect," she said happily. She put the head of the sledge on the ground and leaned the handle against her leg while she pulled her eye protection and work gloves out of her tool belt. Then, finally ready, she gripped the handle and hauled back.

"Hang on," called a male voice.

Jaime sighed and let the hammer's head slide to the ground. Would she ever be allowed to whack the crap out of something on this place? "Hey, Mike," she said. "What's up?"

"Did you get the key out?" Mike Darden appeared from between two lilac bushes. "The guy I bought my place from told me there was a key for your house in that old coop."

"Didn't know anything about it." Although she should have. Almost everyone she knew had hidden a key to their house somewhere. For kids to use coming home from school, for neighbors to check in when owners were gone on vacation, for when you accidentally locked yourself out.

He approached and smiled at her. "Nice hammer."

"Still clean as the day it was made," she said. Pointedly. "Do you know where the key is?"

"Yeah. Right inside the door jamb." He stepped to the tottering structure, felt around inside, and extracted an aged key. "Here," he said, holding it out.

She took it and shoved it in her pants pocket. Eventually, she'd change the locks, but until then a spare could be handy. "Thanks."

Conversation lagged. Jaime made no effort to unlag it.

"Well," Mike said, "I guess I'll be going."

"Okay." She nodded. "Thanks for telling me about the key."

"No problem. Just want to get along with my neighbors, right?" He smiled.

"Right." She picked up the sledgehammer. "See you around."

"See you," he echoed, and slowly ambled back to his house through the shrubbery.

She hefted the sledgehammer, hauled back . . . then put it down.

Because Mike, the good-looking neighbor—Mike, the hardware store guy—knew all about the spare key. He, along with Roger and Bob and Henry, could have gone inside the house any time he wanted.

Mike had to go on the suspect list.

Chapter Nine

That night, Jaime told Lara about her day, including learning that Mike Darden had access to the house. "And I talked to Roger today," she said. "He seemed . . . upset when I told him it was Cilla we'd found."

Lara looked up from her laptop. "Did he know her?"

She shrugged. "My guess is he knows her parents." Roger knew basically everyone in town between the ages of fifty and assisted living. "I told Detective Scoles about who had access to the house, but he had all those names already." Then she remembered. "Well, other than Mike. Do you think I need to tell him about that?"

Lara went back to her computer. "Probably ninety percent of people in Green River have keys or access codes to their neighbor's houses. I doubt it's news to him, but if that conscience of yours is going to kick up a fuss, then you should tell him."

Jaime nodded and used her phone to email a quick note to the detective.

Lara gave her a look. "What are you leaving out?"

"What I had for lunch. Terry's Tacos food truck was out by CS, and this time I'm sure the shrimp is my favorite."

"Right." Lara squinted at her. "Okay, I know there's something you're not telling me, maybe more than one something, but I'll give you a pass on that. For now. What I want to know is progress points," she said, tapping her keyboard. "We need metrics. Quantitative data."

"And what would that look like, exactly?"

"We have house access as a column in our spreadsheet. Yes for Roger, Bob, Henry, Mike, and a maybe for Natalie. I've made new columns for motive, alibi, and personality traits. And by that," she said before Jaime could ask the question, "I mean traits that could lead to murder. Chemical dependencies. Instances of violence."

"Plus," Jaime said, "there's the house itself. Did the killer know I owned it? Or did he think Henry did? Maybe ownership of the house is irrelevant, and the killer simply took advantage of a vacant house, but we shouldn't assume that."

"Good point." Her friend typed so fast it sounded like Morse code.

"You really think this will get solved with a spreadsheet?" Jaime got up to look over Lara's shoulder.

"This is no different than the whiteboards they use on TV shows all the time. No, I take that back. It's better because we can filter and sort."

Jaime hoped she wasn't going to start talking about pivot tables. "Looks like I have a lot of work in front of me. Any idea how I should go about getting any of this information out of people?"

"You'll find a way." Lara shut her laptop. "You always do."

Jaime wasn't sure about that, but when she got up the next morning, she had an idea. "Momentum," she said to the steaming shower water. "That's what I need. The Big Mo. All I have to do is get started."

By the time she was dried and dressed, though, Lara was already gone, so she didn't have a human presence to help with the idea testing. She could have texted or called her, but that just wasn't the same, so she hiked up her metaphorical big girl panties and headed out.

But first, she needed breakfast. She and Lara had worked out a food purchase system over the months she'd been staying there.

Food was purchased on an individual basis, and they alternated coffee responsibilities. Which meant that since she'd emptied her box of cold cereal the day before, she now had to stop elsewhere for morning sustenance.

And oddly, her uncharacteristic lack of planning was turning an annoyance into an opportunity. Or at least a prospect for an opportunity, because she'd come up with an idea that could combine breakfast with information gathering.

She got in her truck and hooked a left turn. One good thing about working in construction was a deep and wide knowledge of the best gas station food available, and Hugh's Quick Stop, just outside of town on River Road, had excellent biscuits and gravy.

Her tummy was already halfway to happy when she pulled into a parking spot and jumped out. She was almost at the front door when she heard a slight thump.

"Hey!" a man shouted. "What do you think you're doing?"

Jaime turned. A girl, who looked almost old enough to have had her driver's license for a week, was sliding out of the driver's seat of a huge and ancient SUV. When she hit the ground, her knees almost buckled.

The voice hadn't stopped yelling. "You backed right into me! Did you even look in your mirror?"

"I—I did," the girl stammered. "I'm sure I did. I just . . . just didn't see . . ." She walked toward the back end of her rusty vehicle with wobbly steps, her face white. "I'm so sorry, I just . . . just . . ."

"Sorry?" the man roared. "I'll see you sorry. Do you know what you backed into? A 1967 Ford Mustang! I just finished restoring it last month. Last month!"

And that's when Jaime realized she'd seen the red-faced man before. The day before, to be exact. It was Warren Brookshire from Carolina Semiconductors. Cilla's boss from CS.

"How—how much damage is there?" the girl squeaked out. "I'll pay for it."

"Darn tootin' you will," Warren shouted, looming over the girl, leaning forward, hands on his hips. "Times two, for pain and suffering!"

That's when Jaime had enough. She walked over, smiling. "Good morning," she said. "Do we have a problem?"

The girl sniffled. "I—I didn't mean to. I was trying to get around the car in front of me, so I backed up a little and I'm sure I checked the mirrors, but—"

"She ran straight into me!" Warren shouted. "Kids don't pay attention these days."

"Let's take a look," Jaime said soothingly, and inserted herself between the man, who had to be six feet tall and well over two hundred pounds, and the girl, who might have been five three and half his weight. "She wasn't going very fast. Perhaps there's not much damage."

The three of them peered at the Ford's front bumper. Then they inched closer and peered again.

"Oh no." The girl pointed at the shiny chrome. "There's a scratch. Do you see it?"

Jaime leaned closer. "I think so." But her voice rose, making it almost a question.

"That was there before." Warren scowled and crossed his arms. "You got lucky, little girl."

The kid nodded, gave Jaime a quick scared smile, scurried away, and in seconds was driving off.

Jaime turned to ask Warren a question about where the scratch had come from, but he'd stomped back to his car and slammed the driver's door. The engine growled to life, and the tires screeched as he peeled away and onto the road.

So Warren was a hothead and a bully, two things for Lara's spreadsheet. Which wasn't proof of anything, of course. But how far away was it from berating a scared teenager to killing a troublemaking employee? Although why would he know anything about the house, let alone the location of the key? And there was a great big empty spreadsheet cell in the motive column.

Back in high school, she'd read that there were actually only three real motives for murder: money, sex, and power. All other reasons could be boiled down into one of those three. Warren was a top executive at an international company. Did he already have enough money and power, or did he want more? There were so many things she needed to find out, and she had no real idea of how to do that. But there was one thing she could do, and she was about to do it.

Jaime went into Hugh's, filled a foam clamshell container with two biscuits, ladled on gravy from a massive stainless-steel pot, and paid by the pound for her breakfast at the front counter. She hadn't seen any King Contractor trucks outside, even though it was just before starting time, so odds were good no one was at the site down the road.

Her earlier idea, which had seemed so brilliant not even an hour ago, had been to "accidentally" run into Henry at the regular crew morning stop. But if he wasn't here . . .

She sat in her truck and forked in her biscuits and gravy, going back in her memory to the morning routine she and Henry had shared for so many years. By now, she would have been out of the house and at the closest job site, checking on progress. Henry, slower to rise, would be checking emails and opening his first Diet Coke of the day.

"I am not going to the house," she said to the steering wheel.

She could text Henry to set an appointment, or even call, but she didn't want to make the meeting a big deal.

It gave her skin a creepy crawly feeling to realize that she was semi-seriously suspecting that the man she'd been married to for fifteen years was a murderer. For so long she'd loved him unconditionally and blinded herself to his now-obvious faults. But . . . had those faults led to murder?

TV shows and movies were always saying that anyone could kill, given the right set of circumstances. Was that really true? Jaime didn't know and wasn't sure anyone did.

Either way, she wanted to get her life in order. Getting back to work on the house was the best way to do that, and even if Detective Scoles thought she should stay out of police business, there was no harm in asking Henry a few pointed questions.

Then a quiet thought wormed into her head: *No harm, unless Henry is the one who murdered Cilla.*

She shoved the thought away, then sighed and let it come back.

What was her true motive in confronting Henry? To exclude him as a suspect, or to make certain he was one? Or was her motive more self-centered, to find the murderer as quickly as possible so she could get back to work? Or, third possibility, was her motive more about Cilla herself, to do what she could to bring a killer to justice?

Jaime swallowed the last biscuit bite. Self-introspection wasn't really her jam. She liked to do things, not think about them, which was why construction—and demolition, its younger sibling—was the perfect career for her.

She collapsed the foam clamshell with a satisfying crunch and slipped out of her truck to drop it in Hugh's nearest trash can. As she opened the small swinging metal door, she saw a familiar white pickup truck pull in.

Once again, procrastination had paid off. Life was indeed improving.

Bob McNinch and Henry got out of the truck and headed to the entrance. They both caught sight of her at the same time and had equally opposite reactions.

"Twice in two days," Bob said, grinning. "How did I get so lucky?"

They bumped knuckles. "Still waiting for that pie," she said, smiling, then looked over at the man she'd once been married to, who was scowling and sidling past. "Henry, do you have a second?"

"What for?" He was almost to the store's front door.

She reached out and gave the elbow of his light jacket a small tug. It was a gesture born from years of habit, so familiar to them both that it took her a moment to realize how out of place it now was.

"Uh, sorry." She sounded like Roger. "Right. Won't do that again, will I?" she said, putting on a smile.

He'd stopped and now heaved a huge sigh. "Jaime—"

Whatever he had to say, she didn't want to hear it. "It's about Cilla Price."

"What about her?"

Jaime was paying close attention. He'd never been one of those guys who looked women in the eye, preferring instead to focus his gaze on other parts of their anatomy, but now he wasn't even doing that. Now, he was looking at the gas pumps.

"You said you didn't remember her," she said. "And that's a flat-out lie."

"What are you talking about?" he asked harshly. "You have no idea what I know and what I don't know. You always underestimated me."

She snorted a laugh. "More like I overestimated you. Because I thought you'd actually remember the girl one grade ahead of you who was voted homecoming queen, class president, and Most Likely to Succeed. I mean, seriously, Henry? Not remembering Cilla Price is like not remembering the name of the street where you grew up!"

His face turned a curious shade of red, then went white.

Uh-oh.

"Leave me alone."

He spoke in a low tone that raised the hairs on the back of her neck.

"Leave me alone," he said again. "You're out, do you hear me? Leave Natalie alone. Leave Bob alone. Leave King Contractors alone. Don't come near any of us ever again." He flung the glass door open and stalked inside.

Jaime, shaken, backed off until she thumped into the ice machine. Had that really just happened? Had Henry threatened her?

"Hey, girl," Bob called, "you all right?"

"Fine," she said, vaguely waving one hand. "All good."

She wasn't, though, and she wondered if her tenacious streak of curiosity had finally landed her in waters she couldn't navigate. Her grandmother had told her many times that being curious wasn't a trait of a lady. For each time she'd been told that, she'd been tempted to respond that polite women rarely made history, but since she hadn't wanted to get her knuckles rapped, she'd kept quiet. Had that been where her tendency to keep her real self buried had started? Way back then?

She closed her eyes briefly and pushed it all away.

That was then, and this was today. She was a grown woman, answerable to no one but herself. No matter what forces had brought her to this point, she was now free to find her own path.

* * *

The run-in with Henry left her unsettled and restless. She'd planned to work more on filling in Lara's spreadsheet blanks—motive, alibi, etc.—but given the mood she was in, there was no way she'd be able to be efficient. What she needed most in the world right then was something simultaneously physical and productive. What she needed was some hammer-swinging time. Luckily, she had just the thing in mind.

Not many minutes later, she was marching across the lawn of the house, baseball cap on her ponytailed hair, tool belt buckled around her hips, work gloves and eye protection in place, and her snappy new sledgehammer in hand.

After a quick duck into the shed to check on the cat—no feline in sight, but she'd have to resupply its food and water before she left—she headed to the chicken coop. Last night, thanks to her neighbor's interruption, she hadn't had time to finish smacking the coop apart into bits. At the time, it had been annoying, but post-Henry, she was glad to have some smacking still to do.

Jaime walked around the small coop, studying what was left standing. One of the four rickety side walls remained upright, and the full weight of roof structure was leaning on it. All she had to do was make sure the roof rafters didn't fall on her head when she kicked out that last wall.

She grinned. Easy-peasy.

With her sledgehammer in both hands, she balanced on the balls of her feet, standing sideways to the coop, aiming all her attention at the corner stud. She hauled back, sliding her hands together at the base of the handle and, smiling, started the swing forward.

"Good morning!" a cheery voice called.

She let the sledgehammer's head drop to the ground. Again.

Mike Darden emerged from the shrubbery. "Coffee?" he asked, holding out two travel mugs. "This one's with cream, this one's black. And I have sugar packets in my pocket if you want some."

More than anything, she wanted to take down the wall, but she was under-caffeinated, and the wall could wait a few minutes. "Sure," she said. "With cream is good." She leaned her sledgehammer against the solitary wall and murmured thanks as she took the mug.

"Heard you pull in," Mike said. "I was making coffee anyway, so I just made a little extra. How's it coming?"

It would come along a lot faster if she didn't get interrupted every time she turned around. "This won't take long," she said. "It's really just something to do until they let me back in the house. I have a proposed renovation timeline, but right now it's only guesswork."

Mike smiled. "Old houses are like people, right? You don't know what's on the inside until you spend a lot of time with them."

Now that was an interesting comparison. Jaime sipped her coffee—which was very good—and thought she might borrow the phrase.

"Randy told me you used to be part of King Contractors," Mike said.

She froze. "Used to be. That's right."

"Right. So you know all about demolition and renovation. This is a great area of the country for that. Old houses are everywhere you look."

For the first time, Jaime wondered about Mike Darden. "You're not from here?"

He laughed. "The accent didn't give me away? No, I get it. Some locals have one, and some don't."

"Depends on lots of things." Family, friends, profession, travel. Her own accent was mild; Lara's had vanished over the years. Henry's was inconsistent; her mom's and dad's were pure Carolina.

"Sure," Mike said. "But I'm from southern Arizona. An old house out there is anything more than thirty years old."

Jaime glanced at the chicken coop. "I think the newest patch on this thing was nailed up thirty years ago."

"Demolition is fun, isn't it?" Mike smiled. "I'm sure you have lots of friends and contractors to pull from, but if you need a hand, just let me know. I'm no finish carpenter, but I'd be happy to help with the grunt work."

"Thanks." She nodded. "Not sure how things are going to go yet, but I'll keep that in mind." She drank the last of the coffee and handed the mug over. "And thanks for the coffee. Have a good day."

Mike stood still for a moment. "Sure. You too. Have a good day, I mean."

Not waiting until he was gone, she turned away, lifted the sledge, and aimed at her target with a laser focus. Nothing was going to interrupt her this time. Nothing.

"Mmww!"

Jaime looked around. Crouched in the edge of the shrubbery was the cat.

"Hey," she said softly, dropping the hammer. Again. "Is he gone?"

"Mww," it said.

"Sorry, I don't speak cat." She crouched down and made clicking noises. "Let's talk deals. I feed and water you until I find your owner, and you keep an eye out for nosy neighbors."

The cat crept an inch closer. "Mww?"

"Well, him, mostly," she said, nodding in the direction of Mike's house. "Because he seems to be over here a lot. I mean, who volunteers to work on someone's house when you barely know their name? Sure, doing demolition is more fun than humans should be allowed to have, but—"

The cat's ears perked up.

Jaime laughed. "What, you like demolition too? Or is that your name?"

"Mmww!" The cat sat upright, its golden-brown eyes staring straight into her.

"So your real owners are builders too?" She laughed again. "Okay, Demolition. Can I call you Demo?"

"Mww."

Demo stood and walked past her, tail in the air. She watched it headed straight into the shed. She tipped her head, listening, and sure enough, heard the sound of crunching cat food.

Smiling, she stood. As she planted her feet and aimed at the chicken coop, a dark thought snaked to life.

What if Mike was trying to be her friend so he could have open access to the house? What if he was trying to get into her good graces so he could get inside and destroy evidence?

She shook her head and took a deep breath.

Then she aimed the hammer and swung.

Chapter Ten

Jaime was sorting former chicken coop parts into the potentially usable (the small pile) and what she'd have to pay to be hauled away (sadly, the much bigger pile) when she noticed a shiny dark blue sedan pulling up to the curb. No one except law enforcement drove vehicles like that. She stood, rolling her shoulders to loosen muscles that had tightened in the last hour or so, and sure enough, Detective Scoles got out and headed straight toward her.

"Thought I told you no access," he said.

Well, that hadn't taken long. It wasn't even noon. But she was more than ready for this conversation. "*Inside* is what you said, and I'm not inside. So, an obvious interpretation of what you said was no access to the house. As we can both see, we're right here, and the house is way over there." To help, she pointed across the broad lawn.

"Hmm." The detective stood in front of her, crossing his arms and looking annoyed. "That's all true, but you should have checked with me this morning to make sure. A phone call would have worked just fine."

"Sorry." Jaime did her best to look abashed. "Next time I work on a house and find a dead body inside, I'll talk to you every step of the way."

He gave her an odd look. "You expect to find more bodies?"

"I didn't expect to find this one."

"Most people don't," the detective said, "but fair enough."

Jaime glanced at her lumber piles. "Did you come all the way out here to scold me, or did you come out to do some investigating?"

"Two birds, one trip." Scoles smiled. "Efficient, I call it. So. About that key you emailed me about last night."

"It was hung on the inside door jamb of this old chicken coop," she said, gesturing at her demolition heaps. "It's old and tarnished, but it looks like a match to the key I have for the front door."

The detective's attention sharpened. "Was the coop locked?"

"There wasn't a lock on the door. Just a piece of wood that turned." She made the motion with her hand.

"I know the kind you mean." Scoles frowned. "So what you're telling me is anyone who knew about the key could have had access to the house."

"Sure, but it looks old, like someone put it there for a spare years ago and then never used it."

"I'll need the key," he said. "I'll write you a receipt."

Jaime had already made that assumption and, still wearing her work gloves, dug into her tool belt for her key ring. She stopped abruptly. "Do you care about fingerprints?"

"Yes," he said, sighing. "Though it's probably pointless. You've touched it, your email said Mike Darden touched it, and if the key has been there for years, half the neighborhood has probably used it to go inside the place and look around."

She felt a pang of sympathy for the detective. So much of his work must feel nonproductive. "There's something else you should know."

"About Mr. Darden?"

"About Warren Brookshire. Cilla's boss at CS." She said she'd heard reports of Warren and Cilla not getting along, and then told him the story of Brookshire's morning verbal abuse of that poor little high school girl. When she got to the end, the detective nodded.

"Thank you. That's interesting information."

But not, Jaime noted, interesting enough to write down.

"What I'm curious about," Detective Scoles went on, "is any information you can provide that links Cilla Price to people with access to the house."

"Links her how?"

"Any way you can come up with. Those names you gave me—your ex-husband, his foreman, your attorney, and now Mike Darden—did any of them know Ms. Price?"

"Oh. Well." Jaime shifted from one foot to the other. Speculating about Roger and Henry's possible guilt had been easier when it had been more theoretical. "Far as I know, Roger didn't know her at all. Henry and I went to high school with Cilla, but like I said before, she was older than we were."

"Just one year older than your ex-husband, correct?"

A detective who knew what he was doing was a good thing, for sure, but it made her insides squirm a little to know he was poking around in the lives of people she knew. "That's right."

Detective Scoles studied her. "Anything else?"

She shook her head, shrugging. "Not that I can think of."

"Hmm."

He stood there, watching her, and her insides squirmed some more. Finally, she broke and said. "If I come up anything else, I'll let you know, okay?"

"You do that, Ms. Moore." He gave her a sharp nod and headed back to his car, ignoring the house completely.

Which meant, Jaime realized, that when he'd said he'd come out there to do some investigating, what he'd meant was he'd wanted to investigate *her*.

For the next hour, Jaime did what she could to finish taking apart the former chicken coop, all the way down to handling, one by one, each piece of potentially salvageable wood. She unscrewed every screw and pulled out every nail and staple. At the end, she had a small but tidy pile of wood and a couple of ideas. There were some wide planks that would make a great kitchen table. And the narrower pieces would be fantastic as picture frames. Maybe she'd take before and after pictures of the house, frame them up, and give the set to the new owner.

Of course, the hard part of those ideas was to actually do them. Once a project got going, it was hard to do anything other than jump from task to task, trying to get everything done at the exact right time to keep all the other tasks flowing along in the right sequence. One little task undone could make the whole thing come to a screeching halt for days or weeks, every hour of which cost money. Which made it hard to remember anything that wasn't a critical part of the process.

Just the thought of it made her smile. She loved renovation. It was an exquisite dance. It was plate spinning. It was a coordination of time, materials, and people that culminated to satisfy one of the most basic human needs: a home.

"There is nothing else in the world that I want to do," she told her small pile of wood. New home construction was great for many contractors, but for her it would always be a distant second. There was something about bringing a house back to life that fulfilled her like nothing else. But could she run a business by herself? Lara would say yes. But did she want to?

"Mmww?"

She jumped. The cat now known as Demo was sitting on top of the big pile of wood.

"Was that a question?"

"Mmww."

So, not a question. It had actually sounded more like a criticism. "It's lunchtime for me," she said. "How about you?"

Demo gave her a long look, jumped off the wood pile, and vanished.

It was becoming obvious to her that cats were not the same kind of creatures that dogs were. It was surprising they even shared the same planet. But as an unintended consequence, she was starting to understand all those cat memes she'd more or less ignored over the years.

Back to the lunch dilemma. Since she hadn't done any grocery shopping, there was no lunch to be had. Her restaurant budget was tapped for the month, so it was either go hungry or go to the grocery store. Neither option was attractive. "Buck up and be an adult," she told herself, and heard a distant "Mmww."

"Glad you agree," she told Demo, and headed across the lawn to her pickup.

A Harris Teeter store was closest, on the main road just outside of downtown. She pulled into the parking lot and gave the sitting vehicles a quick once-over. No white King Contractor trucks visible. No little yellow convertible in sight. Not that she would have retreated if either Henry or Natalie had been there, but like her mom always said, *"Forewarned is forearmed."* Or like her grandpop had always said, *"Pick your battleground, then pick your battle."*

Jamie went inside and grabbed a small pushcart, the kind of cart she'd previously thought of as the cart for lonely people but what she now knew was the cart of efficiency. She started in the produce section, adding what fruits and vegetables she knew for sure that she'd eat, then rolled toward the back for her carb of choice: artisanal sourdough bread.

She was studying the loaves, slightly varied in size, trying to judge the absolute best shape for her future sandwiches, when her attention was caught by a conversation one aisle over.

"Cilla Price? Really?"

"You hadn't heard? Oh, Brittany, I'm so sorry. I thought you knew."

Jaime inched closer. The two women sounded youngish.

"Oh, I heard she'd been killed," Brittany said. "I just didn't know that Natalie knew her."

"What? Nat couldn't stand her. It was because of Cilla that Nat didn't get that customer service job she wanted out at CS."

"Ashley, are you saying that she had something to do with Cilla's murder?"

"What?" Ashley gasped. "No—! All I'm saying is I saw Natalie and Cilla in front of the bakery a while back, and Nat was really laying into her. A one-sided catfight, if you know what I mean?"

Jaime did. But there had to be more than one Natalie in Green River. Maybe they weren't talking about the one she knew.

"Next thing I knew," Ashley was saying, "Nat told Cilla she'd pay for what she'd done, then she jumped into that convertible of hers and took off. She went on a long social media rant about it, didn't you see? It was between a pic of a quinoa salad and a Cosmo. You'd think now that she's living with Henry King, she'd let a little thing like not getting a customer service job go, but that's Nat, right?"

Jaime rounded the end cap. "Hi. Sorry—I didn't mean to eavesdrop, but I overheard what you were saying, about Natalie and Cilla Price. Would you be willing to tell that same story to a detective?"

It turned out that Ashley might—just maybe—talk to Detective Scoles as long as he called her when she wasn't busy or working.

"But maybe not?" Ashley said, her voice rising in a question. "I don't want to get Nat into trouble. I mean, it's not like she had anything to do with Cilla being, you know, dead. They had this argument, that's all. Nat probably has one every day with someone."

Jaime nodded—she could easily imagine that someone with Natalie Blake's sense of entitlement got into frequent confrontations—and asked Ashley to think about it. "We all want to find out what happened to Cilla," she said. "And you never know what small piece of information might lead to finding a killer."

"I guess?" Ashley looked at Brittany, who shrugged. "I mean, it might be okay to talk to a real detective."

After a little more wishy-washiness, Ashley finally agreed that it would be okay if Jaime gave Detective Scoles her phone number. "But I'm, you know, out a lot, so I might not answer right away."

Jaime assured her that the detective understood busy schedules, and thanked her for her time.

She drove back to the house. Her plan for the afternoon was to transport the pile of good lumber to her parents' house, where her dad had already said she could work on projects in his workshop, and start on a design for the kitchen table.

"Was I ever that self-centered?" she asked, thinking of Ashley, as she walked past the shed. She'd caught a glimpse of a gray tail in the doorway, though it had whipped away when she'd approached. Fine with her. It wasn't as if she really wanted a cat. Still, it wasn't horrible to have a creature to talk to, even if it was a cat that didn't understand a word she said.

"Mmww," came a distant voice.

Grinning, she pulled on her work gloves and hiked up her work pants as she crouched down for the biggest planks. The "lift with your legs" maxim was one she took seriously. She'd seen far too many workplace injuries that could have been prevented if the people involved had not assumed that their testosterone made them invulnerable.

"Think this is the house?" Jaime overheard a voice say.

Still crouching, Jaime turned her head. An older couple had parked on the street and were climbing out of their sedan. Both were wearing shiny zip sweatshirts and jeans that bore the telltale signs of elastic waistbands.

"Run-down Victorian house at the end of the cul-de-sac," the man said. "That's what the site said."

"Well, I don't know about the Victorian part, but it's sure run down." The woman cocked her head. "Going to take more than one can of paint to fix up this thing."

Jaime stood, not sure what offended her more: that someone didn't recognize a classic Queen Anne home when it was right there, or that they'd called her house run down. In need of repair, sure. And she'd accept ill-maintained. But the term *run down* summoned images of broken windows and missing shingles, and that just wasn't true. Not as of last week, anyway. "Can I help you?" she asked in a loud voice, striding across the lawn. She reached into her pants pocket for her Swiss army knife. Not that she'd need a weapon, but it didn't hurt to have one ready in case of emergency.

"Oh!" The woman started and put a hand to her throat. "My goodness! I didn't know anyone was here!"

"Can I help you?" Jaime asked again.

"Is this the house where that body was found?" The man was holding his phone up and snapping photos.

Not a body, she wanted to say. A kind and thoughtful woman whose life was cruelly cut short had been found in her house. But she didn't want to say anything more than she had to, so she pointed at the police tape. "The property is an active police investigation. And even if it weren't, this is a private construction project."

"Oh, bother," the woman said. "So we can't see the wall?"

"No," Jaime said. "You can't."

"How about when the police are done?" the man asked. "Think the owner will let us inside then?"

"Don't see that happening." Jaime smiled thinly. "The owner can be a real pain."

The woman sighed. "Well, darn. We were hoping to be the first ones to post interior pictures of this place."

"Post?" Jaime asked. Then she reheard what the man had said earlier. "Hang on. This house is mentioned on some website?"

"You bet. Creepymurders dot com." The man adjusted his mesh baseball cap and smiled. "This murder house is the latest entry."

Jaime flinched at the thought of her house getting that kind of notoriety. "Hate to disappoint you," she said, "but it's not really a murder house. The body was discovered here, but the murder happened somewhere else." At least she hoped so.

"Really?"

"Like I said, it's an active investigation, but"—she shrugged—"that's what they're saying." And it would definitely be what she and Lara would be talking about in a few hours, and the two of them were as good a "they" as anyone.

The couple trudged with slumped shoulders back to their car.

Jaime watched them go, hoping that she'd never see them again. But even if she didn't, odds were good others would be along soon, walking around where they didn't belong, gasping with horrified pleasure, and gossiping about Cilla.

She didn't like the idea. Not one single bit.

Chapter Eleven

Jaime slid the last of the wood into the bed of her truck. A significant length hung out the back end, so she used two sets of ratchet tie-down straps to secure the load. She rooted around in the toolbox for her staple gun—in the bottom, naturally—and stapled short lengths of bright orange plastic flagging to the ends of the wood.

She pushed and tugged on the load, making sure everything was solidly in place, then climbed into the driver's seat and headed for her parents' house. Halfway there, partway through her mental review of what she could remember of Lara's spreadsheet, she decided to take a short detour.

Half of the aging strip mall was occupied by businesses "on the edge"—a consignment shop, a dingy pizza place—and the other half was occupied by an empty storefront. The parking spaces in front of Roger's office were empty, just like normal. Roger's car wasn't there, which was fairly unusual, but Donna Neely's sporty two-door sedan was.

Perfect.

Jaime pushed open the streaked glass door and poked her head inside. "How's the world's best office manager doing today?"

Donna, who'd passed traditional retirement age half a decade ago, lowered the newspaper she was reading and blew out a thin stream of vaping mist. A few years earlier, Roger had put his foot down and forbid her to smoke cigarettes in the office ever again. The next day she'd sashayed in with a bright pink vaping device and given her boss of thirty years a long look that clearly said "this far, and no further." Roger had opened his mouth, closed it, and walked away.

At least that was the story Donna told. Jaime had never asked Roger his version and probably never would.

Now, in a gravelly voice Donna said, "Best office manager, my aunt Fanny. False praise really scrambles my eggs. What do you want?"

"That's what I love about you. No small talk."

"If you're looking for Roger," Donna said, "he's out working on client relations."

Jaime grinned. "At the city golf course, you mean?"

"He sure ain't schmoozing anyone at the country club." Donna snorted. "That man's cheaper than a two-dollar—"

"Anyway," Jaime cut in, "it's you I wanted to talk to."

"Yeah?" Donna folded the newspaper and dropped it on her desk. "What's up, honey? You got man trouble again? You came to the right place." She put up her hand and patted her solidly red curls. "But I got to warn you, my advice comes at a price. Got good news for your wallet, though. Happy hour down the block starts at four."

Jaime smiled. Donna had been trying to set her up on dates since she first came in to talk to Roger about the divorce. "Nothing like that, sorry."

"Well, shoot. And here I was hoping Mr. Neely would have to sit home wondering what happened to me." Donna sat back and put her ankles up on the corner of her desk.

Though Jaime had never met Mr. Neely—had never even learned his first name—she hoped she would someday. Any man who could keep Donna happy for that many years was someone worth knowing.

"If you're not here to talk to Roger, and you're not here for man talk, what's left?" Donna asked. "Because cute as my grandbabies are, I don't expect you want to see their new photos."

By this time Jaime had pulled around one of the two visitor chairs—furniture she'd always suspected Roger had picked up on the side of the road when a hotel was doing renovations and put out the old stuff in hopes that someone would take them and save the cost of having them hauled away—and sat facing Donna.

"It's about Cilla Price," she said. "You've heard, right?"

Donna tipped her head back and looked at the tiles of the drop ceiling, stained with years of Marlboro smoke. "I heard. Yeah. Heard that you're the one who found her too." She slid her gaze in Jaime's direction. "How you sleeping?"

"Fine," she said automatically. And it wasn't a complete lie. The night before she'd slept for three straight hours before the nightmares woke her. "I ran into Roger yesterday. When I told him who it was in the wall, he got weird. Seemed way more flustered than normal."

"That follows."

Jaime watched Donna blow a vaping mist ring, something she'd been told was flat out impossible. "It does? Why?"

Donna blew another ring. "Because Cilla Price used to be one of Roger's clients."

"She"—Jaime's mouth opened and shut a few times and eventually came out with another word—"was?"

"Yes siree. And no asking what she was a client for. I'm okay with losing my best office manager status for telling you Cilla was a client, but there's not a chance I'll open the files and tell you what she hired Roger to do."

"I wouldn't ask that," Jaime murmured.

"Yeah, I know. Just saying." Donna looked at her. "But I'll tell you one more thing. I said she *used* to be a client. That's not because she was killed. It's because about two months ago she fired Roger. And she's been posting things about Roger on those review websites."

Jaime listened to Donna ramble on about the reviews, some of which sounded a lot like what Jaime herself had often thought about Roger's appearance and professional skills, but after she thanked Donna for her help and headed back into the April sunshine, there were two thoughts that she kept coming back to.

Roger's law practice had, to her, always seemed to be on shaky ground.

Which made Cilla's bad reviews a motive for murder.

* * *

Jaime walked around the back of her truck, checked to see her load of wood was still secure, and got inside. The knowledge that Roger had a real motive to murder Cilla wasn't anything she'd wanted to learn.

She tapped the steering wheel and thought about her parents. More specifically, what her parents were likely to be doing at that minute. She had to tell them something, but there wasn't any possible way she'd tell them her darkest suspicions. Roger had been her dad's best friend since they were three years old. Later on, if more evidence piled up, she'd have to tell them, but now? Not so much.

Her skin was itching from the inside out with the need to do . . . something. Anything. It was as if all the weeks she'd spent on Lara's couch had caught up to her at the same time. She could almost feel the pent-up energy roiling around inside of her, looking for a way to get out.

She had no idea where her energy had gone during those dark, sad weeks of winter when it took all of her will to summon the momentum to shower, dress, and feed herself, but she was exceedingly glad the dreary tentacles of depression had released their grip. For a while, she hadn't been sure she would ever feel like herself again.

However, feeling like herself meant physical activity. She needed to move. To do something.

She thought of all the times her mom and dad had suggested, gently and otherwise, that getting a college degree would be the best investment she could ever make. They might be right, but the idea of so many hours spent in a classroom, hours spent studying, hours writing papers, all those hours sitting, sitting, and more sitting—

Shaking away the image of walls closing in on her, she turned the ignition. Time to move. If she couldn't do anything else, she'd take a scouting drive. It had been months since she'd done that. Though Henry had worked the property purchases, she'd usually been the one to find the prospects. Even in a town of less than twenty thousand people, there were always houses to find.

Sure, she didn't have the capital right now to finance a purchase, but if she could get back into the house soon, she'd be on schedule to put it up for sale in less than a year. Timing was everything, and Jaime didn't have enough fingers and toes to count how many times a casual chat with a homeowner or neighbor had resulted in an eventual project. What she had to do was plant a seed in fertile soil, then step back and let it grow.

Finding the most fertile soil was part of the fun. Mindful of the wood behind her, she started a slow cruise near Green River's downtown. Sometimes she skipped the solid areas, knowing it was unlikely she'd pick up a tired house in a stable neighborhood, but she also knew anything was possible. After all, a house could quickly deteriorate for any number of reasons. A change in ownership. An absentee owner. An owner who didn't have the finances for maintenance. You just never knew.

She scanned houses left and right, not seeing anything that jumped out as a strong possibility. A couple of maybes, though, so when she rolled to a stop sign at Center Street and waited for the traffic to clear, she pulled out her phone and tapped in the addresses.

As she slid her phone back into the side pocket of her work pants, she frowned. A bright yellow convertible turned past her. One of the driver's skinny little arms was sticking up, making wild gestures for her to pull over.

Jaime watched in her side mirror as Natalie made a screeching stop in front of a house—one of the houses whose address Jaime had just put in her phone—and got out of her car, wearing those pointy high heels.

A white panel van pulled up behind Natalie's car, and two men in black T-shirts and jeans got out.

Jaime watched, puzzled, as two men from the film crew stood in a tight group with Natalie on the sidewalk. Natalie talked and laughed and smiled at the men, touching their arms every so often. Though Jaime couldn't see the men's faces, she assumed they were smiling and laughing back.

Had the Chamber president hired Natalie to work with the film crew? Jaime couldn't fathom that happening, but the world was a weird place. Or maybe Natalie and Henry were filming some of their jobs for an advertisement. Though that made sense, it sounded expensive.

Shaking her head, Jaime drove off, not sure where she was going, but any place would be fine as long as it was Natalie-free.

* * *

An hour later, Jaime was still driving. She'd added a few more possible addresses into her phone, along with notes on her first thoughts about how to plant the seed of a future sale. She was sitting at a picnic table in a park, one of those small neighborhood spots too small to be a destination for anyone who didn't live in the area, but big enough for a basketball court, a few pieces of playground equipment, and her picnic table.

Late July, she figured, would be a good time to start some conversations. Hot and humid, with four more months of lawn mowing on the horizon, could make almost anyone wonder if moving to a nice new condominium with central air might be a good idea. She'd just added the addresses to her calendar when the phone started ringing.

Detective Scoles. Interesting. She thumbed to accept the call. "Detective. What can I do for you?"

"Ms. Moore, I have a fair amount of information I can release. Would you have time this afternoon to come in?"

Jaime felt a jolt of excitement. Maybe they'd found the murderer, and it was no one she knew, and she could get back to work on the house. "How about ten minutes from now?"

Accordingly, ten minutes later she was sitting in a chair across from the detective and the deputy whose name she couldn't remember. She inched forward and did her best to be surreptitious as she peered at his name badge. Hoxie, that was it.

The detective propped a digital tablet on the table and tapped its surface a few times. "We now have a probable cause of death."

"Probable?" Jaime echoed. "Other than the obvious, what does that mean? Are there ranges of probability, like from sort of probable to really probable? Or are there percentages?"

Detective Scoles glanced up from the tablet. "When bodies are significantly decayed, we're often lucky to get even a probable cause. There are times the remains are so—" He stopped and shook his head. "Probable means just that. Probable. The back of Ms. Price's skull has a pattern that correlates with enough blunt force trauma to cause death."

Involuntarily, Jaime put a hand to the back of her own head. "So it really was murder?"

"That remains to be seen." More screen taps. "Although unlikely, the cause of that trauma could be accidental. However, what happened to Ms. Price remains after her death was most certainly not accidental."

Jaime was not at all sure she wanted any more information. Forensics and medical examiner details weren't anything she really wanted intimate familiarity with outside of the occasional TV show to warp her expectations of reality.

"Not accidental," she repeated, giving Deputy Dave a quick glance. He didn't look any happier than she felt. "So you know how she got into my house?"

"At this point, no," the detective said. "But what we do know is where the remains were between her death and transportation to your property."

The deputy's expression was an odd mixture of fascination and what looked like nausea. Jaime was getting a bad feeling about what was coming. "Do I get three guesses?"

Detective Scoles paused, clearly not having expected that response, then ignored her question. "After running a number of tests, the medical examiner concluded that the remains had been put into a kiln."

"A . . . kiln?" Jaime felt her mouth hanging open and did her best to close it. "Like in pottery class?"

"Accelerated heat is the only mechanism by which the remains could have been transformed to the state in which you found them."

Jaime had the fleeting thought that her high school English teacher would have had a field day diagramming that sentence. "So a kiln. Seems like that would narrow down the suspect list quite a bit."

Detective Scoles made a gesture that was almost, but not quite, agreement. "Our inquiries have expanded in that direction, yes. We have also learned, within a few hours, the most likely date and time of her death. She had a seat on a March sixteenth red-eye flight to Los Angeles, return ticket March twenty-fourth. She checked in with her cell phone ahead of time, drove to the Charlotte Airport's long-term parking, and vanished. Unfortunately, camera coverage of that parking lot is limited. She was seen in one camera crossing the parking lot, pulling a medium-sized piece of wheeled luggage, and wasn't picked up by the next camera."

"A vacation," Jaime murmured. She tried to remember what Ann Marie had said. That Cilla had taken a vacation and never come back. Only it wasn't that; Cilla had never even left. "To visit some friends."

"Correct," Detective Scoles said. "Her cell phone hasn't been used since the check-in and cannot be tracked."

"So sad," Jaime whispered, because she had to say something or she'd start crying.

"Yes," the deputy said quietly. "It sure is."

The three of them sat there for a moment. Finally, Detective Scoles stirred. "With the exception of the main floor, you are now free to work inside the house."

"But—" Jaime stopped herself. Yes, the main floor was the bulk of her work, but there were other things that could get going. Like the upstairs. Like getting into the crawl space and determining the full extent of the termite damage. "Okay. Thanks. I don't suppose you have any idea when the main floor will be clear?"

"The forensics team expects to complete their report next week. They want the wall left alone for now, in case they have to do a follow-up."

It made sense. She didn't like it because she needed to get started on the massive job that was designing and making the kitchen cabinets, but she could live with another couple of weeks. Not so bad, considering.

Jaime thanked the officers and walked out. She could get back to work. Sort of. But it wouldn't feel right, given that Cilla's murderer was still running around.

She hadn't known Cilla that well in high school, and had barely crossed paths with her as an adult, but she knew one thing—she was the person who'd found her body.

Cilla had been tossed aside. Disregarded. Dismissed. Thanks to Henry, Jaime had had a taste of what that felt like. She wouldn't be able to live with herself until she'd done everything she could to get justice for Cilla.

Chapter Twelve

Jaime backed her vehicle up her parents' driveway. Halfway to the house, she saw her dad come out the front door, a coffee mug in one hand, a newspaper in the other. Instead of helping her navigate, he stood there, reading what she assumed was the sports page.

With no directional assistance whatsoever from the man who'd been instrumental in her birth, she braked to a stop, turned the engine off, and got out. "You could have helped guide me in," she said, coming to the back and unlatching the tie-down ratchets.

He sipped what Jaime knew was decaf coffee and tucked the newspaper under his elbow. "Didn't look like you needed it."

As she'd been driving full-ton pickup trucks, forklifts, skid loaders, and the occasional rental cherry picker for more than a decade, she absolutely didn't need his help, which would have been more hindrance than true assistance. Both of them knew this to be true, but that didn't stop either of them from enjoying the moment.

He nodded at the pile of wood. "From your house? Oak."

"I'm thinking of making a planked kitchen table."

"Quarter sawn?"

"Looks like. How's the dust collector working?"

He snorted. "Long as you don't want to use the remote, it works just fine."

Jaime hid her smile. Her dad was forever tweaking the dust collection system, a spaghetti-like network of galvanized pipe attached to the ceiling and every tool in the shop bigger than a screwdriver. But it was worth it. Turn on the collector itself, which was housed outside, and the subsequent whoosh of air meant you never had to sweep sawdust off the floor. That her dad had to turn the system on and off at the wall switch, instead of using the key fob remote that had been fussy ever since he'd bought it, irritated him something fierce.

They pulled on work gloves and hauled the wood down the garage stairs that led straight to the basement. "Have I ever mentioned," her dad said, "that this stairway is why I wanted to buy this house?"

Only about ten thousand times. "Not today," Jaime said. "Thanks for letting me bring my wood here."

"No problem, as long as you're done before school lets out. I have plans for projects all summer long. So," he said, eying her down a ten-foot length of oak that was probably older than both of them put together, "if you keep up this contractor stuff, what are you going to do about tools? You need a workshop. Somewhere to store materials."

She had no idea. "Working on it." And she was, because now that he'd put the idea in her head, she was thinking about places to pick up used quality work tools. A table saw. Drill press. Band saw. Radial arm saw. All that. Estate sales? Maybe. Or one of those big auctions. She could store here, on a temporary basis, anything she bought, but if she was going to make a go of her own renovation business, she needed a home base.

And, she suddenly realized, she also needed a new company name. Renovations by Jaime? Green River Renovations? Ugh. Surely she could do better than that. And better than the very boring King

Contractors. Back when that name had been proposed, Henry and his patrician father wouldn't consider anything else.

Though Henry's dad had never officially been part of the company, Henry had discussed more business decisions with his father than with her. At the time she'd taken that as gospel; it was to be expected that Henry would talk to his dad. Arthur had all sorts of business experience, and she didn't. Now, however, she was flabbergasted at the control she'd happily given away to a man she'd never liked. Or trusted.

Jaime stowed the last piece of wood in the rack. "Thanks, Dad. I appreciate it."

He waved off her thanks. "Nothing but a thing. You staying for supper? Your mom is making pot stickers and shrimp fried rice."

"I'm in," Jaime said promptly. Half days at school often meant her mom had time to make something complicated. Her own plan had been grilled cheese and a salad, so clearly, serendipity was real.

They climbed the stairs, went out through the garage and into the house, and entered a kitchen smelling sublimely of hot oil and shrimp. "Wash your hands," her mother ordered over her shoulder, stirring soy sauce into a mountain of rice. "Then set the table. Food will be ready in ten."

It was only when the pot stickers were gone and Jaime was debating a third helping of fried rice, when her news wouldn't ruin anyone's appetite, that she told them what Detective Scoles had told her, starting with his parting news that a memorial service was scheduled for the following Tuesday, and then telling that what he'd said about Cilla's death.

"A kiln?" her mother asked, frowning. "It would have to be huge for a person to fit inside. Assuming that . . ." Her voice tailed off.

Jaime winced on the inside. "Cilla's body was whole. Not, um, you know . . . in pieces." Her parents looked relieved, and she pressed on. "Does the high school art teacher still use a kiln?"

Her dad, the high school physics teacher, looked at her mom, the high school choir director. "I haven't been in that room in years. Stephany?" When her mom didn't respond, he asked again. "Stephany?"

"Oh!" She started. "Sorry. I was thinking about the art teacher. Nice young man. He's only been with us since September. McKenzie Ross. He's from up in Raleigh," she said to Jaime. "You don't know him."

"Is there a kiln in the art room?" she asked.

"Well, yes, but I don't see how it . . . could have been used like that. It's not the right shape, for one thing. And I doubt it's big enough."

Jaime and her dad exchanged a glance. Her mother had always been spatially challenged. Not once in thirty years had she been allowed to either fill the dishwasher or pack the luggage.

"But there's something you should know." Her mom toyed with her fork. "McKenzie's a wonderful teacher," her mom said. "Isn't he, Brad?"

Her dad frowned. "What are you getting at?"

"This feels wrong." Her mom pushed her plate away.

"Cilla was murdered," Jaime said bluntly. "If you know something, you have to say something."

After a long, quiet beat, her mom nodded. "Yes. You're right. It's just that he's such a good teacher, and you know how a rumor can damage a teacher's reputation." She sighed. "But I'm sure the police will find this out eventually, if they haven't already."

"Find what out?" her dad asked, far more patiently than Jaime could have.

"That McKenzie was dating Cilla Price. They broke up a few months ago." She gave them a troubled look. "And it ended badly."

*   *   *

Jaime and Lara, with Lara's laptop, sat on the apartment's tiny balcony in the last slice of the day's sunshine. Phone weather forecast called for a succession of cloudy and rainy days, and Jaime didn't want to miss out on the last open blue sky she might see for a week. Yes, mostly cloudy meant some sunshine, but nothing could replace a wide-open sky filled with absolutely nothing.

"You're not paying attention." Lara rapped her knuckles against the rickety tabletop.

"Mmm." Jaime's head was tipped back, and she was soaking the light into her skin. It wouldn't be long before the gentle spring sun would become suffocatingly hot, at which point the balcony would become unusable until late September. "Sure I am. I'm thinking about next steps."

"Going inside to reduce our risk of skin cancer?"

"Will another ten minutes make that much difference?" Because that was the amount of time she figured was left before the sun slid behind the apartment building next door.

"Ten minutes today, no. But ten minutes every day of every year of your life—well, that's a different story."

"I promise to wear a hat all day tomorrow," Jaime said lazily.

"Tomorrow it's going to rain."

"Good thing I have a hat to keep the rain off my head, isn't it?"

Lara snorted a laugh. "You must have been a horrible child."

"So my mother tells me." She put her feet on the balcony's railing and leaned back in the white plastic chair, putting her hands behind her head. "How about a summary? A quick rundown of all the suspects and the information we just added."

"Good idea." Lara tapped at her keyboard. "In alphabetical order by last name, we have six on the list: Natalie Blake, Warren Brookshire, Mike Darden, Roger Goodwin, Henry King, and McKenzie Ross."

Jaime silently added her own commentary: Natalie, ten years younger than she was and, on Jaime's bad hair days, ten times prettier;

Warren Brookshire, the ambitious corporate boss; Mike, the neighbor; Roger, the attorney; Henry; and McKenzie Ross, the art teacher.

"We have mostly blanks for motives," Lara said. "Except for Roger."

Jaime didn't want the man she'd called Under Roger for more than thirty years to have killed anyone. "Do we have an alibi column? Because if there's a solid alibi, even the deepest motive doesn't matter."

"Alibi column is already in place." Lara paused. "Anything to enter here?"

"Not yet. But if I get over to Mom and Dad's house before they leave for school, I'll ask Dad."

"In a clever and roundabout way?"

"So roundabout they'll name the next traffic circle in town after me."

"How about the clever part?"

"Not my strong suit," Jaime said, shaking her head. "You'll have to settle for roundabout."

Lara muttered something that sounded like "That man has a lot to answer for," which made no sense at all to Jaime. And then in her normal voice Lara said, "So we have Natalie, who reportedly had an argument with Cilla soon before the murder. We have Warren, a man with bullying tendencies who is reported to have believed that Cilla was a problem employee. There's that McKenzie, who broke up with Cilla not long ago. And there's Mike, Roger, and Henry, who all had access to the house."

"And Bob." Jaime opened her eyes. "The house keys are always in the office, so technically he had access too."

"Sure, but . . ."

Jaime tried not to smirk. Her by-the-numbers, metrics-based, quantitative-over-qualitative best friend was some sort of cousin to Bob McNinch, and she'd said for years that he was one of the best people in the world. How was Lara going to reconcile her instincts with the demands of the spreadsheet?

"Um . . ." Lara pinched her lower lip with one hand, which was a bad sign, but she also started tugging at a strand of her thick hair, something she only did in times of extreme mental duress.

"Tell you what," Jaime said suddenly. "Let's create a new worksheet. Title it something like 'Things We're Obligated to Consider But Know They're Ridiculous.'"

Lara's fingers flew to the keyboard. "Okay, but that's a stupidly long name. How about 'Unlikely'?"

"Works for me." Her eyes closed again.

"By the way," Lara said. "You do realize that Mike Darden is interested in you, right?"

Jaime felt an odd lurch somewhere between her stomach and her collarbone. "Don't be stupid."

"You're the one who's being stupid. No man brings coffee, creamer, and sugar to a woman he barely knows unless he wants to get to know her better in a romantic kind of way."

"He's just being nice. I have something else for the spreadsheet. Do we have a 'Notes' column? This is about Henry."

"Oh?"

Even with her eyes closed, Jaime could tell that Lara's eyebrows had gone up. "Yup. It's the wall, the one where we found Cilla." She suppressed a shudder. "It was painted plaster over cardboard, with furring strips attaching it to the ceiling and floor."

"And?"

"And Henry hasn't swung a hammer in years. Plus, he was never that good at finish work. I don't think he'd have the technical skills to put up a wall like that."

"Hmm."

There'd been a tone to Lara's "Hmm" that meant more was coming. "What?"

"Sounds like a reason to eliminate Henry as a suspect."

"It's factual," Jaime said. "That's all."

"So it doesn't mean you're trying—subconsciously of course—to clear Henry because you still care about him?"

"What?" Jaime sat bolt upright. "You have got to be kidding."

"Hmm."

"Stop that. It's annoying. Okay, I will admit that I don't want a man I was married to for years to be capable of murder, but if he's guilty, he's guilty."

"And that's it?"

Jaime opened her mouth, then closed it. And thought carefully. After a long moment she said, "That's it. There's nothing left, Lara."

"Good to hear."

She nodded. And hoped, way deep down inside, that she'd told the truth.

* * *

The next morning, Jaime was up and out of the apartment before dawn. Lara had headed over to her fiancé's place after the spreadsheet session, and Jaime didn't expect to see her again for a couple of days. She sipped the coffee she'd brewed and knew that the bowl of cold cereal she'd shoveled down wouldn't see her through until noon, not if she was going to be on her feet all day, working.

But that was one big advantage of going to her parents' house to use her dad's workshop. The kitchen was always stocked with snacks for her brothers and their families.

She parked in the street, to stay out of the way of any and all departing vehicles, and went in the front door. "Morning!" she called. "Anyone home?"

Her mother appeared in the kitchen doorway. "Did you eat? And before you say a word, a bowl of cereal is not a proper breakfast. That stuff is half a step above cardboard."

Then again, there were disadvantages. "Thanks, Mom, but I'm fine. I will take more coffee, though." She followed her mother into the kitchen. "Did I tell you I can get back to work on the house?"

"Hmm."

There was that "hmm" thing again. Jaime wondered if Lara had learned it from her mom, or if it just came naturally to some people. "Hmm, what?"

"Nothing." Her mother folded her arms and watched as Jaime topped off her coffee. "It's just that you're going from doing nothing to going all out in nothing flat—that's a big, fast change."

Jaime's mouth flattened into a straight line. For months her mother had been at her to "do something." To come home. To enroll in college courses. To look for a job. To find a new hobby. And now that she was doing something, she was getting criticism? Seriously?

"Restoration is what I love to do," she said, screwing the lid back onto her travel mug so tight it would take a pair of wide jaw pliers to get it off again. "You know that."

"But you've never done it on your own before. Before, you always had—"

Jaime whirled around. "Had what, Mom? Before, I always had Henry around to do the real work? Before, I always had a man on hand to take care of things? Is that what you're saying? That I can't do this on my own?"

"So early, yet so loud." Her dad came into the room, buttoning his dress shirt. "Can you two leave it until I get some caffeine in me?"

"Before," her mom said, with steel in her voice, "you always had crews. A staff. Hands to help. I don't care what gender or shape they are, before you had people to help. I don't like the idea of you being over there alone all the time."

"I know how to do this," Jaime said, biting off the consonants. "I give workshops on construction site safety, remember?"

"Yes, but it's different when you're working by yourself. It's easy to get immersed in what's going on. It's easy to forget to take a safety step."

"I know that!"

Her dad looked at her mom, then at her, then at the space between them. "Well, now that we have that settled, Jaime, let's go downstairs. I have something to show you. Stephany, are we driving together today?"

"Yes," her mother said, not quite snapping, but so very close. "We're leaving in five minutes. I'll be in the car, waiting."

In silence, Jaime and her dad went down the stairs. At the bottom, Jaime looked around and asked, "You don't really have anything to show me, do you?"

Her dad laughed. "There's always something to see in a shop."

A smile crept up one side of her mouth. "Fact." The argument with her mother fell into perspective, easing from a tight ball in her stomach to the soft net of knowledge that her mom wanted the best for her. But speaking of facts . . .

"Dad?"

"What's that, Pumpkin?"

"Not sure I told you yesterday. The police know what day Cilla Price was killed."

"Oh? I suppose that'll help with the investigation."

"It was a Thursday in the middle of March." She went to the workbench, fiddled with one of the bench dogs, and wondered if she'd ever again have her own shop with her own tools. "Dad, I have to tell you something. The police are looking at Roger as a possible suspect."

"Roger Goodwin? You can't be serious. The man doesn't have a mean bone in his body. No possible way could he have killed anyone."

"Sure, I get it." And she did. The idea of Roger lifting a hand to hurt anything larger than a tick was impossible. "But the police don't know that, do they? One of the things they're looking at is access to the house, and Roger had the key." She decided to stay quiet about Cilla firing him and about the bad online reviews.

"Doesn't matter," her dad said. "Second Thursday is poker night."

"How long has that been going on?" Jaime asked idly. "Forty years?" Her childhood sleep had been punctuated by those kitchen table games, ice cubes and poker chips clinking, male voices rumbling in her dreams. Bridge club had been going on almost as long.

He laughed. "None of us are dead. Of course we're still playing. And the games almost always run to midnight, so if that's when Cilla was murdered, doesn't that mean Roger's in the clear? And he's a lawyer, right? Sworn to uphold the law?"

Jaime frowned. Why had her dad made multiple questions out of what should have been a simple statement? He'd sounded like a kid who'd hit a baseball through a window, trying to squirm out of taking the blame.

"And now I have to go before your mother leaves without me." He kissed the top of her head. "Have a good day, Pumpkin."

She watched him walk up the stairs, listened to the door at the top of the stairs shut, and heard the garage door rumble up.

Her dad was the most honest man she'd ever met. He'd taught her from the cradle that loyalty didn't mean anything unless it was backed up by integrity. He'd driven ten miles back to a store to return forty-seven cents of extra change.

So why had he been so weird about Roger and the poker game? What was he not telling her?

Chapter Thirteen

After calling her subcontractors to let them know her project was off pause, Jaime spent a couple of hours in her dad's workshop, feeding the chicken coop wood through the planer to get smooth faces, then pushing each of the long edges through the joiner to get smooth edges. She stacked the results in the wood rack, went upstairs for a quick shower to hose off the fine sawdust that got into her hair and skin despite the dust collection system, then came back down with a fresh cup of coffee and a piece of coffee cake.

She rooted around in drawers under the workbench for graph paper, mechanical pencil, plastic drafting triangle, and calculator. Tools assembled, she took a tape measure from the brown metal Kennedy drawers and measured the now-clean wood, writing down the lengths, widths, and thicknesses on the graph paper.

In the old days, she would have been doing all that to music pouring out of the shop's ancient and massive stereo speakers, but a few years back her dad had scrapped all that in favor of a more modern speaker that was voice activated and had strategically placed tiny speakers that weren't much bigger than her fist.

She activated the speaker as she pulled the metal stool up to the workbench. "Play thinking music," she told it.

The result didn't annoy her, which was all she could realistically hope for, so she let the sounds float around her as she worked out a square footage total. A quick check on her phone gave her standard sizes of dining tables. There was enough wood, and then some.

She tapped the graph paper with the pencil, smiling. The finished table was almost hovering in front of her: wide hardwood planks and solid legs turned on the lathe in a style that would loosely mimic the front porch columns.

Details like that might never be consciously noticed by the home-owner, but Jaime believed, all the way down to her toes, that there was an unconscious recognition of quality, thoughtful design. People who lived in one of her houses would be predisposed to be comfortable. And happy.

The metal stool screeched as she pushed it backward and moved on to the next steps. After cutting biscuit joints, edge gluing, and clamping, she swiped off a bead of overflowing wood glue. "And you're done," she told the future tabletop. "I'll be back tomorrow, okay? Don't go anywhere."

Though technically an hour was all it took for the wood glue to set, with a big project like this she wanted a full twenty-four-hour curing time before working on it again.

Upstairs, she found enough refrigerator contents to assemble a hefty sandwich. She fitted it into a plastic baggie, shoved some potato chips into another baggie, grabbed a soda, and carried it all outside to her vehicle. The dashboard clock told her she had to hurry if she was going to make it to the high school during lunch hour, so she practiced self-discipline and didn't try to eat and drive at the same time. Well, except for a few potato chips.

She pulled into the familiar parking lot and texted her parents a thank-you for the lunch. Then, because the backlash would be horrific if she didn't tell them up front, she added: *I'm at the school to talk to McKenzie Ross. Does he eat lunch in his classroom?*

Dad: *I think so.*
Mom: *Why do you want to talk to him?*
Jaime: *Okay, thanks.*
Mom: *Why?!?*
Jaime: *Tell you later.*

"Sorry, Mom," Jaime said, and turned her phone to silent mode. After she talked to McKenzie, she'd have to give her an answer, but right now she didn't have time, and besides, she didn't know exactly what to tell her.

What she wanted was to get a good look at the school's kiln. Spatial relationships weren't her mom's thing, but they were one of the things Jaime was best at doing. Even Henry had acknowledged that she was far better than anyone else at King Contractors for rough estimates of building height, room sizes, and even ground elevations, which could be very deceiving to the eye. It wasn't anything she'd studied or trained for; it was just a knack she'd always had.

She walked into the building, chatted briefly with the aging security guard who'd known her since birth, and headed for the hallway that led to the art rooms. Though it wasn't a route she'd taken much as a student, she knew they hadn't moved; they were still behind the gym and still full of smells she couldn't identify.

The first of the art classrooms was empty, but in the second a man about her age was seated at a desk, working at a computer with two monitors. She'd pictured him as tall and stringy with a bushy beard and a ponytail. Instead, he looked plumpish and was clean shaven, with hair so short he probably used an electric shaver to cut it.

"Hello?" she asked, knocking on the open doorway. "McKenzie Ross?"

"That's me." He looked up. "Let me guess, your son wants to be an artist, you want him to go into finance, and you want to use my salary as his cautionary tale."

Jaime laughed. "You get that a lot?"

"Not yet, but I haven't been here long." He smiled politely. "What can I do for you?"

"First I need to tell you who I am." She took a deep breath. "My parents are Stephany and Brad Moore."

"Oh hey!" His smiled went from polite to real, and he stood, holding out his hand. "You're Jaime. Good to finally meet you. Your mom and dad talk about you and your brothers and their families all the time."

She groaned as they shook. "Sorry about that."

"No, it's nice." He remained standing and pushed his hands into pockets of his baggy pants. "So what does the daughter of the choir director and the physics teacher need from the art teacher?"

"Well, it's a little awkward, but I think you deserve to know." She hesitated, but Detective Scoles hadn't told her to keep any information to herself, so . . . "It's about Cilla Price."

"Cilla." He sat suddenly and heavily. "I heard the other day. I can't believe it, you know?"

"There's something else. I'm the one who found her."

He gave her a blank look. "You did? But I heard she was in a construction site."

"The house I'm renovating."

"Oh. A house." He nodded slowly. "Renovating. Okay."

Jaime watched him carefully. "I knew Cilla myself, back in high school, so when I heard you two had been dating, I wanted to talk to you in person."

"It was over months ago," McKenzie said. "And we'd only been dating since October, but . . . Well, anyway, thanks for telling me. Knowing it was a Moore who found her makes it . . . a little easier somehow."

Jaime wasn't sure that was true, but it was a kind thing for him to say. "Well, I'll let you get back to work. Lunch is over soon, right?"

Simultaneously, they both turned toward clock above the door. "Six minutes," he said. "Tenth-grade drawing class. I need to . . . get the supplies ready."

Jaime thanked him for his time and left. At the doorway, she looked back. McKenzie was out of his chair, but instead of laying out art supplies, he was standing at the window, his back to the room, hands to his face, and his shoulders heaving.

*   *   *

As soon as Jaime slid behind her steering wheel, she pulled out her cell phone and texted Lara.

> Jaime: *High school kiln far too small to fit a body*
> Lara: *How do you know?*
> Jaime: *Saw it*
> Lara: *Did you take measurements?*
> Jaime: *It's too small—trust me*
> Lara: *Okay*

But even if that kiln was too small, Jaime figured an art teacher would know someone with a kiln that would have been big enough. Artists. Other art teachers. People who sold kilns. All that, however, was not something she was going to think about too much. That was the kind of thing that the detective and Deputy Dave would look into.

Her only intent had been to meet McKenzie Ross and get a feel for what kind of man he was. What was Lara's spreadsheet column? Personality traits? She texted her to enter that he was funny, sharp, and grieving for his ex-girlfriend.

Though she knew that meeting someone for five minutes didn't mean you knew anything about them, she also knew that people tended to judge someone's character within thirty seconds of meeting them.

She'd interviewed enough job applicants to know this was true. And she'd made enough hires, both good and bad, to recognize that she should trust her judgment. Needless to say, her judgment was more about showing up to work on time and knowing one end of a nail gun from the other than murder, but she figured the instinct was a transferrable one.

What she'd learned from the visit was that she would have hired McKenzie Ross. The fact that she'd also managed to take note of the kiln's size was just a bonus.

She sat in the parking lot, ate her lunch at a speed that would have horrified her mother, then popped the top of her soda and headed out. One quick stop at the hardware store, then she'd spend the rest of the day taking measurements, making sketches, and scheduling subcontractors.

All of that was going to take longer than usual because her power computer and her three massive monitors were now considered property of King Contractors. Once upon a time, as her dad kept reminding her, computers didn't exist, and buildings managed to get built, and if they could do it, so could she, because she didn't want to spend what money she had on anything other than necessities. Her only necessities at this point were food and tools, and if she could keep using her dad's woodworking tools for a couple of months—well, every little bit helped.

She parked behind the hardware store and headed in that direction, but decided at the last second to make a quick detour. It had been months since she'd walked into the Green River Chamber of Commerce, and since she was here, she might as well get the final word on that film crew, and why Henry and Natalie were involved. A soft electronic ding warned someone of her entrance. "Hello?" she called. "Is anyone here?"

"Be right there!" said a perky female voice, and true to her word, a fiftyish woman bustled out of a back office and into the front reception area. "What can I help you . . . Jaime! How are you?"

She smiled at Karin Vowell. "How's that kitchen faucet working out?" she asked, and the happy trill of laughter told her everything she needed to know.

"Genius," Karin said, spreading her arms wide and giving her a huge hug. "You are an outright genius. That faucet was just what the kitchen needed, and I'm sorry I ever doubted you."

Jaime emerged from the vast embrace a bit breathless, but grinning. When Karin committed to something, she brought all of her boundless enthusiasm to the table. It had made the renovation project for the house she and her husband bought after their kids moved out one of Jaime's favorites, and it also made her a perfect Chamber of Commerce president.

"So what's new with you?" Karin asked. "Oh, and sorry to hear about the divorce, but you are far too good for that man. He doesn't deserve you and never did."

Jaime murmured something vague about moving on to new things. "I'm working on a house now. If everything goes well, I hope to start my own company."

"It'll go great," Karin said, lightly shaking an index finger, her bright red fingernail waving around in the air. "You were always the brains behind King Contractors. Whatever you decide to do will be a success, and I expect to see you in here at the end of the summer, joining as a new Chamber member."

"Sounds like a plan. But I actually stopped by to ask you a quick question."

"Fire away."

"What can you tell me about the film crew that's been running around town?"

* * *

Jaime went into Gardner's Hardware Store, puzzling over Karin's response: "All I can tell you is what I've been hearing. My favorite is that Steven Spielberg is scouting Green River as a location for his next movie, but it's more likely what Billy said, that a real estate agent from Charlotte signed a big listing and is pulling out all the stops for a big sale."

She'd been so sure that the filming was something the Chamber was tied into. Karin typically knew everything that was going on inside Green River and in all the towns in a twenty-mile radius. If Karin didn't know, who did? Or, more specifically, who might know that she could ask?

It was obvious that Henry and Natalie knew what was going on, but Jaime didn't want to know badly enough to ask those two. She could just see the simpering smirk on Natalie's face. "Oh, you're asking little ol' me?" she'd say, eyes fake-wide. Then she'd giggle and say, "Honey, you'll have to ask your husband . . . oh, dear, sorry, I guess he's your *ex*-husband, isn't he?" Then she'd giggle some more and—

"You been cranky like that all day?" Randy Johnston asked mildly.

Jaime was brought back to where she was and what she was doing. The hardware store. She realized she was giving a display of garden tools a death stare, and smoothed her face into a smile.

"Hey, Randy. Sorry. I was just . . ." She squinted at the man and asked, "Have you seen those guys in a white van? Dressed in black, with big cameras like TV news reporters have?"

He nodded. "Sure, I seen them. What are they up to?"

"I was hoping you'd know. I just talked to Karin Vowell, and she doesn't know either."

Randy scratched his chin, gray with stubble. "Huh. Joey said he heard it was a documentary about haunted houses. Ghosts and skeletons and haints and spooks." He gave her a sideways look. "With that Cilla Price in your house, bet they come talk to you soon."

A haunted documentary made as much sense as anything else and sort of explained why Henry was involved. But she wanted that kind of notoriety for her house about as much as she wanted more termite damage.

"Speaking of Cilla Price," Randy said, leaning against an end cap display of solar yard lights, "if you hear rumors about her and Mike, don't believe them."

Jaime, who'd just decided that Karin was right—the film guys had probably been hired by a real estate agent—blinked at him. "Sorry. What?"

"She'd been seein' that new art teacher, you know, the one with the last name for a first name and a first name for a last name?"

"McKenzie Ross," she murmured.

"That's him. Anyway, it was soon after that her and Mike went out a couple of times. All it was. Nothing more."

After a long moment, Jaime said slowly, "Okay. But why do you think I needed to know that?"

"Just sayin'." Randy shrugged his thin shoulders. "Seeing that you're going to be spending a lot of time at the house next door to Mike, thought you might be interested, is all."

"Thanks, but I'm not interested in Mike Darden's love life," she said flatly, knowing it was an outright lie.

Randy said something that sounded like "Don't believe you," but Jaime was already walking away, headed for the hand tools. She had things to do today, and standing there listening to Randy's gossip was definitely not on the list.

*   *   *

When Jaime got to the house, the first thing she did was trek back to the shed to refill the cat's food and water bowls.

She poked her head inside. "Here, kitty, kitty, kitty." There was no vocal reply, but she did hear a rustle in the back corner. "No need to run out to greet me," she said. "Yes, I'm feeding you, but there's no obligation on your part to show gratitude."

"Mmww?"

"Sure, it'd be nice, but I've heard what cats are like. I don't expect much."

"Mww."

Jaime smiled. She'd loved her dog inside and out, but they'd never had conversations like this.

"Do you talk to Mike at all?" she asked as she opened the cat food bin. "Or am I special?"

The cat tiptoed into the cloudy light coming in through the open door, sat on the dirt floor, and stared at the food bowl, still half full.

"Working on it. You know, I don't care that Mike went out with Cilla," she told Demo. One of these days she'd have to admit to Lara that she'd given the cat a name. But there was no reason to rush these things. And maybe the cat would find its way home before then and spare her the humiliation.

"Mmww?"

"Nope," she said. "Doesn't bother me even a little—"

She stopped and sighed. It was time to stop kidding herself. She liked the guy. He was considerate and nice and funny. To know that he had a connection to Cilla, on top of having access to the house key? The knowledge didn't bother her a little.

It bothered her a lot.

Chapter Fourteen

The point behind buying painter's tape and additional rolls of bright orange flagging she'd picked up at Gardner's was to keep her from forgetting about her hand-on-heart vow to Detective Scoles to stay away from the first floor except for a straight line between the front door and the stairway.

She pulled the stepladder she'd borrowed from her parents' garage out of her truck, carried it inside, and averted her eyes from the warning sign about not standing on or above this step, figuring that since she weighed less than half the ladder's capacity, that somehow made up for it.

But if she'd seen any of her employees doing the same thing, they would have instantly been hauled into the office for a stern hands-on-hips lecture, been shown videos of people falling off ladders, and been forced to listen to a quiet statement to the effect that if they were ever caught doing that again, she'd have to let them go.

Hypocrisy was a horrible thing.

She sighed. "Sorry, Mom," she said in the general direction of the high school. "Soon as this is done, I won't do it again." She taped one last long streamer of flagging to the ceiling, climbed down, and looked at her handiwork. Long vertical strips of inch-wide plastic tape, spaced every couple of feet, were draping down from the ceiling to knee level. Not anywhere close to a true barrier, but since all she needed to do was stay out of the rest of the first floor, she figured this would work just fine.

"And now," she said with satisfaction, "I can get busy."

She practically bounded outside to get what she needed from her truck: retracting tape measure, folding wood rule, mechanical pencils, stud finder, and clipboard with the pad of graph paper she'd borrowed from her dad's shop.

Starting in the attic, she measured, sketched, and took photos. She started with the ceiling height, which was far easier to do by yourself with the nice stiff folding rule than with the retracting tape measure that had an amazing capacity to be flexible when you least wanted it to be. Then she moved onto the window shapes and sizes, window locations, room size, and stairway location. She wasn't sure she was going to do anything with the attic other than clean it, but part of the process was to create accurate drawings of the entire house.

Idly, she wondered if anyone at King Contractors had picked up any training on ArchiCAD, the building information modeling software she'd used for years. Without access to that program, she was having to go back to the basics of pencil and paper, but that was okay. Henry had been the one to insist on purchasing the software. Though it had been fun to learn and use, the cost was far more than she could justify at this point.

As she worked her way down to the second floor, she occasionally thought about Lara's spreadsheet. About the people on it, and why they were on it. About the many blanks yet to be completed. And about how she'd find the information to fill in those blanks.

She thought about it as she measured the four bedrooms, and continued to think about it when she sat on the floor of the second-story's single bathroom, sketching in the locations of the toilet, sink, tub, and associated piping.

"Mmww."

Jaime looked up from her clipboard. The cat was sitting in the exact middle of the doorway, the white tips of all four of its paws peeking out. "Well, hello. How did you get in here?"

Demo didn't answer.

"Please tell me I left the front door open just enough for you to sneak your way inside."

Still no response.

"Because otherwise there's an entry point that's big enough for a cat. And if it's big enough for you, it's big enough for more than cats." For squirrels and possums and all manner of creatures that didn't belong inside the house.

Demo blinked once.

"Is that once for yes, twice for no?"

Two slow feline blinks.

Jaime laughed. "Okay, I can see where this is going." She stood slowly and inched toward Demo. "Hey, there," she said soothingly. "Kitty kitty kitty. You're not huge, but you're way too big to get in through any of those teensy-weensy foundation cracks, and—"

She stopped abruptly, coming to a reluctant, and in retrospect, a very obvious conclusion. This must have scared Demo, and he jumped up, rotated a hundred and eighty degrees, scrabbled for traction on the floor, and pelted down the stairs

Size mattered. Natalie Blake was short and petite. And she was not, if the muscle tone of her upper arms and how she'd been slightly winded putting shopping bags in her car's trunk were an indication, inclined toward vigorous physical activity. Besides the fact that she probably didn't have the skills to put up the wall, how likely was it that she had the upper-body strength to move the weight of a full-grown woman?

Natalie couldn't have done it.

And Jaime still had no idea who had.

* * *

Jaime strategized her Sunday arrival at her parents' house with the precision of a military operation. Too early and she'd be the first one there and would face the full force of her mother's questions. Too late and she'd be the last one there, and all eyes would be on her: Mom's, Dad's, her three brothers', their wives', and the eyes of every single overly curious niece and nephew.

Her goal was always to arrive after Allen and his family, but before Caleb and Evan and their families. Her ultimate goal was to walk in the door *with* one set of the nieces and nephews, otherwise known as the "double N's," because that would divert attention from her and onto the grandchildren.

This Sunday, her luck was mixed. She parked on the street—always did, to avoid the horrific possibility of being blocked in the driveway—and took a car count.

Four. Allen, Allen's oldest son, Allen's oldest daughter, and Caleb and his wife. No Evan.

Her current options were to hang out in her truck until Evan showed up, or to go in by herself. She studied the house and saw the kitchen curtain twitch, which effectively eliminated the staying-in-the-truck option, because the delay wouldn't be worth the questions she got from her mother.

She got out of her vehicle and shut the door, went back and shut it again, because it didn't hurt to make sure it was shut tight, and then fortune smiled on her.

Beep beep!

Evan's shiny four-door pickup eased into the driveway. "Hey, Sis!" he called out his open window. "Want to lend us a hand?"

Of course she did. Smiling, she opened the back door and started unpacking two-year old Robby from his car seat.

"I can do it!" he said, pushing at the buckles with his stubby little fingers.

"You know that," Jaime whispered loudly, "and I know that, but your Mommy and Daddy don't. Let's keep it our little secret, okay?"

"Okay!" he shouted, grinning.

"Jaime, you're a blessing," Emily said, detaching their five-year-old from the other car seat while Evan went to the truck's bed for the picnic basket of food and a tote of toys. "But what's the deal with that house? You really found Cilla Price's body?"

"Mom will make me talk about it over coffee, once the kids leave the table," Jaime said. "You could just wait for that."

Emily laughed. "I prefer the raw version."

There was more than one reason Emily was Jaime's favorite sister-in-law. They waved the kids into the house, along with Evan, and the two women stayed outside, leaning against the truck and keeping out of sight of the kitchen window.

Jaime gave Emily a recap of the last few action-packed days of her life. She started with the wall coming down, moved on to not having access to the house, and told her about learning it was Cilla. Then, after having Emily take a vow of silence, Jaime described her list of suspects and Lara's spreadsheet.

Emily listened intently. She was a social worker, employed at a state health center, and was extremely good at listening. At the end, she said, "That's a lot to take in."

"I know, right?" Jaime sighed. "From top to bottom, the whole thing is hard to believe. Mostly that Cilla Price was the nicest person I've ever met, other than you, and I hate the fact that someone killed her."

Emily, who normally would have crossed her eyes and stuck out her tongue at the compliment, instead frowned, creating a small vertical line between her eyebrows. "I have to tell you something you're not going to want to hear—and stop putting your hands over your ears." She paused. "The poker game ended early last month."

"It . . . did?" Jaime pictured the four men at the table: her uncle Terry, Roger, Emily's dad, and her dad.

"Had to have. You know my parents are taking care of my sister's kids for a while, right?"

Jaime knew that Emily's brother-in-law had been diagnosed with cancer. Though his prognosis was good, the effects of the chemotherapy were knocking him down hard. "Sure. How's he doing?"

"Better. But that night one of the kids was running a fever, vomiting, the whole nine yards. Mom called, I went over to help, and Dad got home before eleven because your uncle Terry got called out on a fire department run. Can't believe he's still volunteering at his age."

The front door opened, and Evan's head poked out. "Hey, you two. Mom told me to get the both of you inside or suffer the consequences."

Jaime and Emily exchanged a glance, then levered themselves off the truck and headed into the crowded, noisy, boisterous, biweekly family event.

But for once, Jaime wasn't doing her best to maneuver a seat at the extended table, equidistant from her mother and her oldest brother, because she was trying to recall exactly what her dad had said about the poker game.

"The games almost always ran until midnight," he'd told her. He'd given Roger an alibi. Only that game had ended early, and now Roger's alibi was gone. Had her dad forgotten? Or was he covering up for his best friend?

"Got a seat for you here, Pumpkin." Her dad pointed at the chair next to him.

She hesitated, then sat down.

Chapter Fifteen

Lara listened to Jaime's recitation of the events at the Moore's Sunday dinner table, then took a long drink from her glass of iced tea. "I'm never sure," she said, "if I'm envious of your compulsory Sunday dinners or thankful that my family has scattered and the only times we're subjected to meals like that is Thanksgiving, Christmas, and Easter."

"You're welcome to join in," Jaime said. "Bring Tony. It would make a change from the regular Jaime interrogation."

That day had been no different from so many others. Once the table was cleared of the meal, the oldest grandchildren served the adults dessert and coffee and took the younger ones out back to play. As soon as her dad's fork cut into the pie crust, the questions had started, beginning with one from her mother—"So what's this I hear about you and Mike Darden?"—and ending with her brother Caleb's comment, "That table top is going to warp if you don't take the clamps off."

Because she'd completely forgotten about removing the clamps, she'd snapped out, "At least I know how to edge glue without ruining the workbench," which had made Allen and Evan laugh and Caleb's ears turn red.

All things considered, Jaime decided, it had been one of her better comebacks. Not that anyone was keeping score—though for years there had been a tally taped to the refrigerator, their mother had taken it down when Evan graduated from high school—but there was no feeling equivalent to smacking down an older brother with a quick comment.

"So how," Lara asked, "does your mom know anything about Mike Darden?"

Jaime had wondered the same thing. "When I asked, she just smiled and said mothers see all and know all." She rolled her eyes. "Dad said they'd stopped at the hardware store after school to pick up a new aerator for the bathroom sink. Mike was there, and they got talking."

What Jaime hadn't liked, after her mother had described Mike's good looks, was the hooting from her brothers and the sly glances from her sisters-in-law. The last thing she needed at this point in her life was any distractions or complications, and a romantic relationship with the guy next door to her project house qualified as both.

But it hadn't helped at all that when her mother talked about Mike, she'd felt her face heat up. "Aunt Jaime's blushing!" a young nephew sang out, giggling.

Even now, sitting in the apartment with Lara, she felt her cheeks start to burn. She buried her face in her iced tea and drank long enough to feel the red fade.

"Anyway," she said when she surfaced, "Dad may or may not be, um, stretching the truth about that poker game, but either way, Roger doesn't have an alibi. And he has motive. Not sure anyone else really does." She had to face the reality that Roger was a top suspect, and reality had rarely been so unappealing.

"Well." Lara kicked off her shoes and put her feet up on the coffee table. "I learned something, but I'm not sure if it has anything to do with Cilla's murder."

"Learned what? From who?"

"Tony." Lara slid into a comfortable slouch. "You know how he visits restaurants and grocery stores all over the region?"

Jaime nodded. Lara's fiancé was a supply chain analyst for a food wholesaler. He watched the ebb and flow of purchasing trends, tracked delivery times and order sizes, and kept in close contact with a wide range of store personnel, from store owners to janitors. Tony had the sharpest memory of anyone Jaime had ever met, and she'd long ago learned to tag him as her partner in any game involving trivia.

"I was talking to Tony about all this"—Lara pointed her toes at her laptop, open to the spreadsheet—"and he said he knows Warren Brookshire. Turns out Brookshire is not only the head guy at CS, but he's also a partner in the Corner Bar and Grill, that new restaurant out by the expressway."

"Really?" Jaime had been inside once, to meet her brother Evan for lunch. The food had been decent, but the whole place had a sports theme and had three times as many televisions as it did windows. She'd felt vaguely claustrophobic the whole time and was not inclined to return.

"At least he *used* to be a partner," Lara said, raising one eyebrow.

"What do you mean? That place hasn't even been open a year, and it's packed all the time. How could it be going under?"

"It's not, as far as I know. And before you ask, they don't bank with us, and even if they did, I couldn't tell you anything about their statements."

Jaime nodded. Lara's position at the bank meant she signed confidentiality agreements more often than she blinked.

"What Tony told me," her friend went on, "is that Warren wants to cash out of the partnership. The other partner was talking to Tony about it because to pay Warren off, he needs to suddenly come up with a wheelbarrow of money, and he was hoping Tony could extend the grace period for their upcoming food order."

"Huh." Jaime thought about that. "Did the partner say anything about *why* Warren wanted out?"

"Just that things had changed."

"Huh," Jaime said, more slowly this time.

"Exactly. Kind of makes you think a little, doesn't it?"

"There's only one problem," she said.

"Yup." Lara nodded. "The restaurant doesn't have anything to do with Cilla."

"Correction. Doesn't have anything to do with her as far as we know. It's possible something about the restaurant is connected to Cilla. We just don't know what."

"So we haven't actually learned anything," Lara said, sighing.

"Not true. We know something happened in Warren Brookshire's life to trigger a change. What we don't know is whether or not it's connected to Cilla's murder." She stood and stretched. "I'll call Detective Scoles tomorrow and tell him about the restaurant. Figuring out this kind of stuff is his job, not ours."

"Theoretically," Lara said. "But who's going to care more? You, who knew Cilla, who found Cilla, and who is trying to get a renovation business going, or a cop who needs to arrest someone to keep his boss happy?"

Jaime frowned. "What is it with you and Scoles? Is there some history there I don't know about?"

"How did it get so late?" her best friend mused, looking at her phone. "No, I never met him before that day at your house. Will I see you in the morning, or are you out at 'oh dark thirty'?"

"I'll be out before eight," she said. The sky was starting to show signs of light long before seven, but Jaime wasn't jumping out of bed at five in the morning, not for now. The early bird got the worm and all that, but she needed to pace herself. She'd gotten out of shape over time; getting back in would have to go the same route.

Lara went off to bed and Jaime unrolled her sleeping bag, wondering when she was going to push her friend about Baxter Scoles. Lara had been patient with her, and was still being patient, so she'd return the favor and wait until Lara was ready to talk.

She began drifting down into sleep and spent most of it planning a trip to Warren Brookshire's restaurant.

* * *

The next morning, after talking to a number of her subcontractors, trying to make sure she hadn't lost her spot on their schedules, Jaime stopped by the sheriff's office. She asked to talk to Detective Scoles and was told he wasn't in.

"Can I leave a message?" she asked. She did, in the form of a voicemail through the lobby phone. She ended the short tale about Warren's sale of his restaurant partnership share with "Um, well, that's about it. If you have any questions, you, um, know my number." She hung up, feeling like an idiot, and remembering why she avoided leaving voicemail messages.

She left the sheriff's office and headed to her truck, hands in her pants pockets.

"Good morning," said a male voice.

She stopped abruptly and turned. The voice had been calm and polite, and other than Henry's or Natalie's, it was the last voice she wanted to hear. "Arthur," she said politely to a silver-haired man wearing a suit, tie, and carrying a leather briefcase. "Nice day."

Henry's father gave the sky a raking glance. "I suppose it is. What are you doing here?"

She smiled because she no longer had to try to pretend that she liked him. He'd never cared for her, accusing her of convincing Henry to go into construction instead of following his footsteps by getting a law degree and a private practice. "That's none of your business," she said, and started to walk away.

Stepping into her path, he said, "If it has to do with my son, it is entirely my business."

She squinted up at him. "Don't know if you noticed, Arthur, but these days nothing your son does has anything to do with me."

"You found Cilla Price's body," he said.

"And?"

"You vowed revenge on Henry. I will not let you drag his name through the mud. Slander is a crime punishable by law."

Something was off here. Something was going on that Arthur was worried about. Luckily, Jaime knew just how to push his buttons. She laughed out loud. "Henry's not bright enough to know the difference between slander and sludge."

Arthur put his purpling face way too far into her personal zone. "You breathe one word of Henry's recent involvement with Cilla Price, and I'll slap you with a lawsuit so expensive you'll never crawl out of debt." He whirled and strode toward the entrance of the courthouse.

Jaime took deep breaths. In. Out. In. Out. After a few rounds, she relaxed her hands, which had turned into fists.

So Henry and Cilla had been involved recently?

How very interesting.

*　*　*

Jaime was halfway to the house when her phone rang. She glanced at the screen and saw that it was Detective Scoles. She pulled over to a nearby curb and parked.

"Detective," she said, "what can I do for you?"

"Just wanted to thank you for the information," he said. "We will be looking into Mr. Brookshire's activities."

"Do you think he murdered Cilla?"

"Ms. Moore—"

"Sorry," she said, cutting in. "I know you can't talk about an active investigation. It's just . . . well, somehow I feel responsible."

"Are you saying you killed Ms. Price?"

Jaime's eyes went wide, then she heard a snort of laughter through the phone. "That wasn't funny," she said loudly.

"Sorry about that," Detective Scoles said, sounding sincere. "Didn't mean to upset you."

She blinked at his apology. He was admitting that he made a mistake? That he was, in fact, a human being made her a little uncomfortable. "Anyway," she said, "can you tell me what you've learned about kilns? It's just I got curious because my parents work at the high school, and the one there isn't anywhere near big enough for . . . for that."

"Yes," Scoles said. "It's turning out that only commercial pottery kilns are large enough for a human body. But the greater difficulty is the temperature. Generally speaking, most commercial kilns don't have a setting low enough to create the conditions found in Ms. Price's remains."

Jaime thought about that. "So what now?"

"Now?" the detective repeated, a bit tersely. "Now Deputy Hoxie and I will spend time wearing out our shoe leather. Thanks again for the information, Ms. Moore."

He clicked off before Jaime could say, "Have a nice day." She squinted at her phone in its dashboard holder, then turned it off. It had been nice of him to call at all, she supposed. He didn't need to do that. And the information about the kilns was interesting, for sure.

She pictured the detective and the deputy traipsing all around Perkins County, looking into kiln ownership. Then, if they didn't find anything, into Charlotte, up into Winston-Salem, over to the Blue

Ridge Mountains; and then, exhausted, dropping down into South Carolina.

It sounded like a huge job, and Jaime felt some empathy. But as far as she knew, there was only one way to tackle huge jobs. Get to work.

"Speaking of work," she murmured, and drove herself to Beason's Lumber. But instead of pulling into the loading area, she walked into the main office, where Doug Beason was pouring a pound of sugar into his coffee. How the man still had all his teeth, she had no idea.

"Back again?" he asked. "Don't tell me you cut up all that ply-wood already."

"In my dreams," she said. Someday she'd have her own crew again. Not for this project and maybe not this year, but soon. "No, I'm wondering about old wood. The house I'm working on is pushing a hundred and fifty years, and I'd like to match what I can. What do you have in that back barn?"

"Hmm." Doug leaned back in his creaky office chair. "Good question. Haven't been back there in a couple of weeks."

For Jaime, the back barn at Beason's was the best thing ever. Doug, now that he'd handed over most of the daily operations to Sami, his daughter-in-law, had time to indulge in his hobby of architectural salvage. If he caught even a whiff of an old house being torn down or renovated, Doug would do his Good Ol' Boy thing, and soon the back barn would be packed to the rafters with doors, hardware, wainscoting, trim, windows, fireplace mantels, and—every once so often—pieces of raw lumber that made Jaime salivate.

"Want to take a look?" Doug sipped his coffee.

Jaime itched to grab the barn key from the hook and run, but she knew she had to do this on Doug time. "Sure," she said. "If you don't have anything else going on."

"All I got these days is time." He yawned and stretched. "But you got things to do, so come on."

They left the office and started across the lumberyard's loading area, where Sami and her favorite forklift were loading a full bunk of studs onto a car-hauling trailer. Beason's delivered, but some people, such as Jaime, preferred to save the money and haul their own.

Sami nodded at Jamie. "Hey, Doug!" she shouted over the motor's *chug chug chug.* "Did you call in that order for two-by-fours? KD. We have plenty of the green wood."

Jaime stopped.

She was so stupid.

Pottery kilns were not the only type of kiln in the world, not even the only kind of kiln in the county. She'd known that for most of her life.

Because *KD* stood for "kiln dried."

Chapter Sixteen

Sami Beason took her baseball cap off and swatted it against her thigh. Sawdust flew in every direction, but Jaime had already anticipated what was coming and stepped out of range. "Come again?" Sami asked, settling her cap back onto her short-cropped blond haircut. "You want to know about what?"

Since Sami was a few years older, she and Jaime hadn't crossed paths in high school, but they'd forged a solid working relationship. If the circumstances were right, Jaime had a feeling they could be good friends, but for whatever reason, the right circumstances hadn't yet developed.

Maybe now was the time, Jaime mused. She was back to work and free of Henry's—and Arthur's—expectations. Maybe now was the perfect time to venture out into the world and find new friendships. Certainly some of the old ones weren't working any longer. Almost all of the couples they'd done things with had been Henry's friends, not hers, the only real exception being her brothers and their wives. Funny, she'd never noticed that before.

"Lumber kilns," Jaime said to Sami. "Do you know anything about them?"

"In theory, sure." Sami laughed. "Build a big box, stack in some green lumber, heat it up. Come back later and take out dry wood."

"How about in practice?"

Sami tipped her head. "You thinking about getting into the lumber manufacturing business? Because we could always use new sources." She grinned. "Especially if they're cheap."

"No, that's not it, I—" Jaime stopped and thought carefully about her next words. The fact that someone was asking pointed questions about lumber kilns could get around fast because people talked. And if Cilla's body had indeed been put into a lumber kiln, that talk could alert the killer, evidence could be destroyed, and Jaime would forever feel a guilty weight on her shoulders.

She started again. "My dad might be thinking about a small lumber kiln, to use when he retires." Something that could possibly be true because her dad thought about lots of things. She smiled. "Not that he wants to cut into your business—he loves you guys, but he might get into furniture-making a lot more seriously in retirement, and a lumber kiln could make a big difference in profit margin."

Luckily, Sami was buying the story. "Your dad is awesome. If it wasn't for him, I'd still be scared of the Pythagorean theorem. No, I get it. Every penny counts when you're running a business." She glanced around at the lumberyard, smiling faintly, then shook her head. "All I know about lumber kilns is that big commercial ones can cost deep into six figures. But I'm sure your dad could make a backyard one without too much trouble."

Jaime's attention, which had started to wander, came back with a sharp snap. "You can make one?"

"Sure." Sami shrugged. "Look them up online. There's probably a hundred different sets of directions, but I bet you could make a backyard lumber kiln in a weekend."

"How big would something like that be?" Jaime asked slowly.

"Depends on the size of your parents' backyard," Sami said, then laughed. "No, it probably depends more on how much room your mom would let your dad have."

Jaime didn't want to blurt out, *"Would it be big enough to fit a human body?"* So instead she asked, "I'd guess he's thinking about one maybe eight feet long, and maybe three feet tall and deep." The size of a coffin, she realized, and suppressed a shudder.

"Sounds doable." Sami nodded. "I think Lowell Smith made one a few years back. I can ask him to give your dad a call."

"No, that's okay," Jaime said quickly. "I'm, um, actually thinking about making it for him for a retirement present. He hasn't announced, but it'll probably be next year."

"Good for him. So if it's a surprise, do you want Lowell to call you instead of your dad?"

She did indeed, and Sami promised to contact Lowell, who Jaime remembered as being a few years ahead of her in school, memorable for a senior prank that had reached mythic status by the time she got to high school.

As soon as Jaime climbed into her vehicle, she pulled her phone out of her pants pocket and did some quick research on lumber kilns. She called Detective Scoles and had no choice but to hang up or leave a voicemail, so she left a rambling message about lumber kiln temperatures and that if she found out more, she'd let him know.

She hoped Lowell Smith would call her sooner rather than later, and decided that if she didn't hear back within a day or two, she'd stop by Beason's again and see if she could get Sami to call him right then and there and hand the phone over to her.

The rest of the morning she spent double-checking dimensions on her floor plan, following up with her subcontractors, and working on cost estimates and purchasing timelines. This was the fuzziest part of the renovation process: running cost projections before the walls were opened up. Until that was done, there was no way to get solid answers. The best she could hope for was to be in the ballpark, and that the percent she put aside for unexpected costs, the contingency, would be enough.

Her phone dinged with a text just before lunch. It was from her mom, with her dad also in the thread.

> Mom: *I packed enough lunch for three, and it's a beautiful day. If either of you want to share my pulled pork and coleslaw, let me know.*
> Dad: *I can be at our spot in ten.*

Jaime (who hadn't packed anything for lunch): *Be there in fifteen. Thx, Mom.*

Her mother sent back a smiley face emoji, and Jaime felt something inside her unwind. In spite of the fact that she was the baby of the family, and the only daughter, she and her mom didn't spend a lot of time agreeing with each other. Their relationship had improved over the years, but kindred spirits they were not and never would be.

Lunch would be good, though. If nothing else, her mom's pulled pork was fantastic.

At the school, Jaime parked in the main lot, next to a pick-up truck with a bed full of what looked like scrap metal. Steel mostly, she decided, taking a look as she walked by, and she wondered if the price for scrap had gone up enough to make a haul worthwhile. There was metal in the shed, and a few bucks was a few bucks.

She was moving forward but looking back at the truck, and almost ran into a hand-in-hand couple walking her way.

"Sorry," she said, feeling stupid. "My fault. I wasn't—oh. Hey."

"Hey back," McKenzie Ross said, and made the introductions. "Rila, Jaime Moore. She renovates houses and is the daughter of

our choir director and our physics teacher. Jamie, this is Rila Clo-
hessy, an amazing sculptor who moved to Green River from North
Dakota."

She nodded politely at the tall, muscular woman and made the
connection. "Yours?" she asked, pointing at the truck laden with metal
bits.

"In all its glory," Rila said, smiling. "Pieces of junk, but it gets me
where I need to go."

After few more sentences of idle chat, Jaime said, "My parents are
in the grandstands with a picnic lunch, so I better go before my dad
eats all the coleslaw."

Rila and McKenzie laughed, said polite goodbyes, and went their
separate ways.

And on the way down the hill to the grandstands entrance, Jaime
sent Lara a text: *McKenzie Ross is dating someone. He must not
have been all that broken up about his breakup with Cilla, so not
much motive there.*

> Lara: *Forgot to tell you. I tracked down his address. He lives
> in an apartment.*
> Jaime: *So no big kiln.*

McKenzie was off the suspect list.

*   *   *

That afternoon, Jaime and her carry strap moved the sheets of plywood upstairs into the master bedroom. Instead of making cabinets
off-site and having to haul them over, up, and in, she was going to
fabricate and finish them right there.

Henry had always scoffed when she'd tried to make the case for
on-site work, saying that moving wasn't that big a deal, and anyway

151

ordering cabinets was faster, and time was money, so what was the point of full custom work?

For Jaime, the point was complete and utter control of the final product, something else Henry had scoffed at.

Henry, she was slowly coming to realize, had been scornful of a lot of things she'd suggested. And she'd backed down, almost every time.

"Why did I do that?" she asked Demo, who'd oozed inside when she'd propped the front door open to bring in her tools. "Why did I let him take over so much of the decision-making? What made me think my opinion wasn't as valuable as his?"

The gray and white cat gave her a hard stare, sighed, and looked away.

"You know what? You're right," Jaime nodded. "That question should be reframed. It should be what made *Henry* think his opinion was more valuable than mine?"

"Mmww."

Jaime smiled, because that had certainly sounded like approval. Not that she knew for sure, having never lived with a cat, but it sure hadn't sounded like disapproval. "Glad you agree," she said. "And I'll be right back. I left that bag of screws outside.

She was opening the door of her truck when Mike Darden came through the lilac bushes, once again with two paper cups of coffee.

"Hey, neighbor," he said, nodding. "Decaf?"

She hesitated. This was a man on the suspect list. A man who'd dated Cilla and not said anything about it. But being polite was a bone-deep response, so she said, "Thanks," and took the one that had "Cream" written on it.

"What's today's project?" he asked.

"Bathroom cabinets."

"Making them on-site?"

"Soon as I get over to my middle brother's house. He has a table saw he's letting me borrow." She'd sealed the deal on Sunday, after dessert and after promising to attend a year's worth of her niece's home cross-country and track meets. But since Jaime typically tried to attend all of her events anyway, it wasn't exactly a hardship.

"Let me know when you're looking to buy a new one," Mike said. "I can let you know if we have any sales coming up."

Jaime made a noncommittal noise. Caleb hadn't used his saw in years; she was pretty sure she'd be able to hang onto it indefinitely. "Sounds good," she said. Then, to make conversation as much as anything, she asked, "Do you know anything about lumber kilns?"

"Commercial or backyard?"

She should introduce him to Sami. "Backyard."

"Good, because I don't know much about commercial kilns, outside of they're expensive. Backyards, though?" He grinned, and Jaime realized once again how good-looking he was. "How much time do you have? Because thanks to my dad, I can tell you more than you want to know."

"Oh?" she asked.

"Yeah. My dad was a finish carpenter. High-end commercial stuff, mostly. He got tired of buying warped and knotted lumber and figured out that if he got wood for almost free—and you can, if you know enough tree removal guys—he could hire a sawyer to rip it to raw lumber, then dry it and plane it himself, and he'd end up with quality wood at a great price."

It was also, Jaime knew, a lot of boring and repetitive work, but she kept that thought to herself while Mike described his dad's sequence of increasingly bigger and more-complicated lumber kilns. It was clear that, as he'd said, he knew a lot about the operations of the device where Cilla's body had probably been placed.

She blew the steam off her coffee and casually asked, "Have you ever had one? A lumber kiln, I mean?"

"Nope. Like I said, my dad has one out in Arizona, but my own knowledge is purely theoretical. I'm glad I know something about them, though." He shrugged. "It's amazing what people expect the manager of a hardware store to know."

Jaime thought of a question she hadn't thought to ask before. "They figure Cilla was murdered on March sixteenth and moved here not much later than that. Do you remember seeing anything? Or anyone?"

He shook his head. "The police knocked on my door the other day, asking me the same thing, but I was out of town that week. In Arizona, helping my parents move. My story must have checked out, because look." He held up his wrists and grinned. "No handcuffs."

A massive sense of relief washed through Jaime, and she almost laughed out loud with sheer, unadulterated happiness.

Mike Darden was officially off her suspect list.

* * *

The route to her brother Caleb's house took Jaime past the strip mall where Roger had his law office. Jaime made a decision just before the parking area came into view.

"Rats," she muttered, because Donna's car was sitting out front, all by itself, but a decision was a decision, so she pulled into the lot.

"Well, hello, Little Miss Sunshine," Donna drawled, looking up from her cell phone. "What brings you to this neck of the woods? If you're looking for Roger, not sure what you were thinking, because it's near five o'clock. That man hasn't been here this late since Jimmy Carter was in office as a governor."

Jaime knew that wasn't true. Roger worked very hard, albeit sporadically. She also knew that Donna was rock-bottom loyal to Roger but would go to the stake rather than admit so out loud.

She sat in the chair across from Donna's desk. "There's no easy way to say this, so I'm just going ahead. I've heard the police are considering Roger as a possible suspect."

Donna squinted at her. "Suspect as a what? Don't tell me the man got caught going too slow for the speed limit again."

"For the murder of Cilla Price."

After a long moment of hollow silence, Roger's office manager threw back her head and laughed loud and long. "Good one, Jaime," she finally said, patting her chest. "You had me going for a minute. Roger, a murder suspect?" She went off into another peal of laughter, this time ending in a coughing fit.

After she was sure Donna wasn't going to require an ambulance ride, Jaime said, "I'm serious. Roger had access to the house, and with Cilla's negative online reviews, he had financial motive."

Donna reached for a tissue and wiped her eyes. "Good heavens, child. That's no motive for Roger. He wasn't upset because her reviews meant lost business. Most of his clients don't know the first thing about review sites. And if they do, they must not care, because there sure hasn't been any drop off in business."

"Then why did he act so weird when I told him about Cilla's murder?"

"Because he's Roger. He hates losing clients. Takes it as a personal failure."

Jaime was puzzled. "So he wasn't worried that Cilla's reviews might hurt the business?"

"Goodness, no." Donna waved away the concern. "If he was worried, it's because he worries about everything. This practice is as solid as Fort Knox. The man could retire any time he wants to."

"Oh." Jaime wanted to be happy, but she wasn't a hundred precent convinced that Donna was telling her the complete truth. After all, Donna routinely told clients who called that Roger was in court when he was actually playing pickleball. She claimed that was a court, so she wasn't out and out lying. Jaime shifted. "Still, the police might be asking Roger questions. I know he was playing poker with my dad the night Cilla was murdered, but I also heard he left early. Do you know why?"

"He's getting up there in age," Donna said, shrugging. "My guess is he just can't take the late nights like he used to."

Jaime sort of bought that but sort of didn't. And the vague look of concern that she saw on Donna's face made the *sort of* part far bigger.

*   *   *

Jaime backed up into Caleb and Doreen's driveway just after dinner time. Or what would have been after dinner time if she'd kept to the rigid schedule imposed by her brother and sister-in-law. Maybe that kind of thing came with having kids, but she'd always been more inclined to follow the dictates of her stomach than the clock.

"Have you eaten?" Doreen asked, poking her head out the front door of the two-story brick house.

Not for the first time, Jaime wondered if Caleb had intentionally married someone just like their mom, or if it had been a twist of fate. "I'm fine," she said, coming up the walk.

"That means you haven't," Doreen said firmly. "I'll never hear the end of it from your mother if I don't see you eating something. Come into the kitchen and sit down."

Jaime saw no reason for her mother to know anything about the visit unless Doreen and Caleb told her about it, something that was easily avoidable. But she also knew it was easier to go along with Doreen than to dig in her heels. And besides, she was hungry, and Doreen and Caleb were excellent cooks.

A sudden small internal lightbulb flicked on in her head. It had recognized what she'd just thought: that sometimes getting along is easier if you just go along.

Was that what she'd done with Henry since he'd first noticed her in high school? Had she been so flattered that the popular football star was interested in talking to her—going out with her!—that she'd let him swallow her life whole?

Surely it wasn't possible. She was a strong, confident woman who had numerous skills and talents, and one of the side benefits of having three older brothers was that men had never intimidated her. So how had she let her personality be taken over by Henry?

"What's the matter?" Doreen asked, ladling marinara sauce onto a pile of pasta. "You look like you just swallowed a fly."

"Something like that." More like she'd just realized the extent of the damage Henry had done to her. The damage she'd let him do.

"Parmesan's in the fridge. If you want some salad, there's a tub of leftovers."

Jaime rummaged in the refrigerator for cheese, greens, and salad dressing. She set it all on the kitchen counter and took a small plate and utensils from the cupboard.

"Sit." Doreen elbowed her toward a stool at the kitchen island. "You've been working on the house all day, haven't you? Sit and take a load off."

It didn't take much to convince her. As she twirled spaghetti around her fork, she asked about the whereabouts of Caleb and their offspring.

"Fishing," Doreen said.

Jaime tapped the side of her head. "I'm sorry. I could have sworn you said *fishing*." To the best of her knowledge, her middle brother had never fished in his life. Caleb was the least outdoorsy of the entire Moore clan and was famous for mistaking a stick for a copperhead snake. In the backyard. When he was twenty-five.

"Don't ask." Doreen rolled her eyes.

"Happy not to." Jaime smiled.

"So." Her sister-in-law put her elbows on the island and gave her a look. "You going to tell me what's going on?

"Not really."

Doreen laughed. "How about if I swear on my grandmother's pecan pie recipe not to tell a soul? Especially any souls with the last name of Moore and the first name of Stephany?"

Jaime considered this. Doreen was a reporter. She'd worked for the local newspaper ever since graduating from college, and Jaime always looked for her byline. Most of the time she didn't read the articles to the end because Doreen covered local government, and Jaime couldn't work up much interest in city and county budget woes, but still. "Reporters never give up their sources, right?" she asked.

"Pinky swear." Doreen held her hand out, little finger crooked.

Jaime put down her fork, and the deed was done. She had a wisp of a thought, that she and Doreen could actually be friends. They'd always been cordial, but for whatever reason, their relationship had never jelled into anything more. Something else to lay at Henry's feet? Maybe, because he'd always insisted they spend equal time between his family and hers, even though his family consisted solely of his father.

"You're getting that same swallowed-a-fly expression," Doreen said.

There was a reason for that. "I've just realized how stupid I am."

Doreen tipped her head to one side. "And you realize I'm not going to let you beat yourself up, right? You're one of the smartest, most capable people I know."

Jaime blinked. "I . . . what?"

"We've been worried about you for years. You were subsumed by the Kings. Honestly? We're relieved you're not tangled up with them any longer."

Jaime wasn't sure she knew the definition of *subsumed*, but she got the gist. "Truth? That's what I was thinking about, coming in. That

I'd let Henry run my life. If I'm smart and strong, how did I let that happen?"

"Relationships are complicated beasts," Doreen said quietly. "I wouldn't want to guess to the why of any of that. I'm just glad you're out."

"Onward and upward?" Jaime twirled more spaghetti onto her fork.

"Exactly. You deserve better than Henry King."

"Does Natalie?"

Doreen smiled. "I think those two deserve each other."

"Sure, it's just"—Jaime chewed and swallowed—"I heard Henry was seeing someone else a couple of months back."

Her sister-in-law snorted. "So he's cheating on Natalie already? That didn't take long. Do you know who with?"

"Cilla Price."

After a beat, Doreen asked, "They were dating?"

Trying to remember the details, Jaime said, "Pretty sure that's what I heard."

"Oh. Well." Doreen blew out a small sigh. "Honey, those weren't dates."

"They weren't? How do you know?"

"Cilla called me after she came back to town. I didn't know her in school, but we have mutual friends, so we connected."

"But . . . why?"

"When she was out in California," Doreen said, "Cilla was a human resource director for a television network. Don't ask me which one—I can't keep them straight. She contacted me, asking if I knew of any human resource jobs at any of the papers around here, or at any of the TV stations. I didn't, but we got to talking and kept in touch the last couple of years."

Jaime kept quiet, waiting for the rest.

Callie Carpenter

"And a couple of months ago, Cilla asked what I could tell her about Henry King." Doreen quirked up a smile. "I told her everything, of course, but she already knew about King Contractors and about the end of your marriage."

"What did she want to know?" Jaime asked.

"Why Henry would be asking about her network connections in California, and—" Doreen stopped. "You know something."

"Not really." Jaime stared at her plate of spaghetti. "But this week I saw both Henry and Natalie with a film crew."

"Soon after you found Cilla." Doreen looked off into the distance, thinking, then shrugged. "I'd be happy to believe the worst of Henry, but I just can't get those dots connected.

Jaime, however, knew that Henry loved to be the center of attention. She knew that he hated to be wrong about anything, she knew that he would do almost anything to win his father's approval, and she knew he had a temper. If Cilla had come between Henry and a goal of his, Jaime could absolutely see that temper exploding into murder.

Chapter Seventeen

Lara stared at her, then started laughing. "Well, that was unexpected," she said through bursts of laughter. "Are Henry and Natalie trying to be the next big movie couple? What would their combined name be, Natary? Or Henlie?" She slapped her hands over her mouth, but giggles seeped out anyway. "No, wait," she gasped. "I have it. Natry!"

Jaime waited for the howls of laughter to subside. She'd come up with Kinglie, because she knew "King Henry" was what most of their employees had called him behind his back, but Natry was good too.

"Glad this amuses you," she said.

"Oh, it does." Lara wiped her eyes. "It's just too funny thinking that Henry has delusions that he has what it takes to be a TV star."

Since Jaime had no idea what it took to be successful in television, she kept quiet. In high school, Henry had avoided the theater crowd as if they'd carried deadly contagion, and she couldn't remember him ever saying anything about being interested in acting. Then again, he'd been successful at keeping his affair a secret for months, so who knew what else he'd kept hidden?

"And that Natalie." Lara's giggles turned her words into a stutter. "She has the brains of a soggy tea bag and the temperament of a wolverine. Seriously, who would want to work with her?"

Jaime, reading between the lines with her recent conversations with Bob McNinch, was pretty sure he was already tired of Henry's new partner. "She has to have some redeeming qualities. Maybe, she, um, helps her grandmother every week with grocery shopping. Or picks litter off the sidewalk."

"Aren't you the generous one?" Lara reached across the dining table for her laptop. "Natalie Blake wouldn't touch anything she doesn't have to. Too much risk to her manicure. And I bet she hardly ever makes the time to see her grandma. Too busy trying new hair care products."

"This sounds like the opposite of the halo effect," Jaime said. It was something she'd read about when developing techniques for employee interviews. "You know, how if you think somebody is good at one thing, you tend to think they're good at other things. And in case you're wondering, they call the opposite of the halo effect the horn effect."

"Whatever." Lara didn't hold much weight with the soft sciences. She tapped at her computer screen. "So what do we do with this new information, that Henry was asking Cilla about whatever television network she used to work for?"

"Do you think it's important to know what network?" Jaime looked at her phone, far away on the coffee table. "If Cilla's Facebook page is still up, I can probably find it on there. Or I bet she has a LinkedIn profile. That will say for sure."

"Not sure what difference it would make."

Jaime agreed but made a mental note to look it up anyway for the sake of thoroughness.

"What we don't know," Lara said, "is whether Natalie talked to Cilla."

Jamie let her memory drift backward a few days. "Did I tell you I saw Natalie with the film crew?"

"Yes, but all that means is she talked to the film crew. It doesn't mean—"

"Wait." Jaime sat up straight. "Pretty sure I forgot to tell you this. I was at Harris Teeter last week and overheard two women about Natalie's age talking about Cilla."

"Eavesdropping?" Lara grinned. "You go, girl."

"Anyway, if what they were saying is right, Natalie applied for a job out at CS but didn't get it. She blamed Cilla and told her she'd pay for what she'd done."

"Wow." Lara looked at Jaime. "That's a real motive."

"I gave Detective Scoles the phone number of the woman who'd seen Natalie yelling at Cilla, but I don't know if he followed up."

Lara muttered something Jaime couldn't hear, then said, "There's a problem with Natalie as the killer."

"I know. She's so small. No way she has the strength to haul a body around."

They stared at the spreadsheet, as if watching it would formulate some answers. Then something occurred to Jaime, something that previously hadn't entered her mind.

"What if Natalie didn't do it alone?" she asked. "What if Henry helped?"

Lara's brown eyes looked at her, not blinking. Then she nodded and started typing.

"But what we should really do," Jaime said, "is go out for dinner."

Her friend frowned. "You already ate. So did I."

"Okay, not dinner. How do you feel about a deep-fried appetizer?" Because it was time to visit the Corner Bar and Grill and learn as much as they could about its part owner, Warren Brookshire.

* * *

Jaime and Lara walked into the dimly lit restaurant and were waved in by a hostess. "Sit anywhere you like," she said, and they took seats at the bar, their backs to the tables of people looking up at one of the television screens attached high on the walls.

Lara glanced over her shoulder. "You'd think they'd get stiff necks doing that."

"Happens all the time." The bartender, a square-faced man in his mid-forties, smiled across the top of a run of beer taps. "Doesn't seem to stop them, though."

"Get someone in here to do neck and shoulder massages," Jaime said. "One of those chair things."

Lara grinned. "Could be a profitable revenue stream."

The man gave a wry smile. "I could use one of those. Or ten."

Jaime felt a tingle. Could investigating really be this easy? "You own this place?"

"Me?" He laughed. "No, I'm the manager. But I'd love to retire early and spend the rest of my life with my toes in the sand, sipping drinks with umbrellas."

"Sounds good to me," Lara said, sighing.

Jaime gave a sideways sort of nod. Though sitting on a beach was fine for most people, she knew she'd be bored silly at the end of the first morning.

After a quick look at the menu, they decided on fried pickles and sweet potato fries. The patrons behind them were shouting displeasure at a home plate call, so Jaime leaned forward to give their order. The man, whose nametag read "Slam," nodded. "Coming right up."

"Um." She leaned forward a little more. "I heard a rumor that this place is for sale already. Is that true?"

He held out his hand and waggled it back and forth. "Depends on how you look at it. One of the partners wants out. Are you interested?"

"Why does that guy want out?" she asked. "This place is busy even on a Monday night. You'd think there'd be a lot of money to be made."

"No idea." Slam shrugged. "I'm just the hired help. No one tells me that kind of thing. I'd like to say you could get a deal on it, but from what I hear, Brookshire is holding firm."

"Brookshire?" She glanced at Lara, but her friend's attention had been sidetracked by the baseball game. She turned back. "Is that Warren Brookshire, out at CS? I have a friend who works there."

Slam nodded as he typed their order into the bar's computer. "That's him."

"Didn't he just move here a couple of years ago?"

"About that." Slam hit the "Send" button, glanced at the screen, then picked up a pint glass and began to fill it with draft beer. "Said he loved it here as a kid. He had an aunt and uncle on his mama's side in Green River. Spent half his summers with them, some big old house on Holt Road."

The tingle on Jaime's neck was back. "Holt?" she asked. "There aren't many old houses out there. Do you mean the two-story with the big wraparound porch?"

"That's it." Slam put the pint glass down on a tray and picked up another glass. "I hear someone's finally renovating the place." He laughed. "Better them than me. That place has to be a money pit."

Jaime smiled a vague agreement. But what she was mostly thinking was that Warren Brookshire knew about the house—and he almost certainly knew about the hidden key.

*　*　*

That night, Jaime soaked in the bathtub until her skin was like a prune, listening to rain hurl itself against the window and wondering where Demo was sleeping. As far as she could tell, all the times Demo had been inside had been because she'd left the front door open.

Then again, she'd never taken the time to do a hundred percent thorough check for a cat-sized hole. She'd do it tomorrow first thing.

As long as it wasn't raining. Some people were fine working in the rain. She, however, was not one of them. She hated working in wet pants. Hated wet socks even more. It was probably a character flaw, but she'd always been able to avoid working in the rain because rain didn't last forever, and there was always something to do inside, even if it was just cleaning.

The next morning, she struggled out from a mild anxiety dream of forgetting to study for a history test and heard . . . nothing. She blinked fully awake, then stretched and yawned, remembering. Lara was at her fiancé's place. And—

Wait. Nothing? She was hearing nothing?

Jaime fumbled for her phone, knocking it off the coffee table and onto the floor before picking it up.

She tapped open her favorite weather app—a far better app than the one her brothers wrongly preferred—and studied the image floating across the small screen. The past and present rain was off to the east, and the future rain was now tracking north of Green River.

"Perfect," she said, closing down the screen and hopping out of bed. She took a quick shower, put her wet hair up into a ponytail, and pulled on an old ratty ball cap.

She ate cereal and slipped a handful of granola bars into her backpack while she slapped together a couple of peanut butter and jam sandwiches for her lunch. Food needs dealt with, she hurried outside and peered up at the sky.

Cloudy with the feel of rain.

She shrugged and put her trust in the phone app. The rain was gone for now.

But when she said so at Beason Lumber, Doug Beason disagreed. The gray-haired, gray-bearded man with great big gray bushy eyebrows shook his head. The action only slightly dislodged the floppy-brimmed hat that left his head only when he went into a church. "Don't care what your phone says. It's going to rain, and soon."

Jaime checked her phone again, which still showed nothing. "You going to call a time?"

He grinned around the toothpick stuck into the corner of his mouth. "Nine fifteen. Count on it."

"If it rains at nine fifteen," Jaime said, putting her hand on her heart, "I will put an ad in the newspaper that you were right and I was wrong."

"Make the type nice and bold." Doug said, then nodded at Sami, up on a forklift. "Hey, partner! We need to get ready to get a nice frame for Monday's newspaper. Going to be a big announcement in it."

Sami Beason nodded. "Whatever you say, Doug. Now will you get out of the way so I can put Jaime's wood in her truck?"

Doug chuckled, stepping over the old railroad tracks, once upon a time used for lumber delivery to the yard, and in short order, Jaime was on her way to Gardner's Hardware with plywood hanging out the back of her truck. She'd strapped it down, but plywood was slippery stuff, and she didn't want to drive around with it any longer than she had to, so she was taking as direct route as possible to the house.

She walked into the back of the hardware store. Fasteners were all she needed. Wood screws. Some deck screws. And what she really needed was a small compressor and nail guns, but she was still hoping to find someone who was getting out of the business—or the hobby—and was looking to sell their stuff cheap.

Maybe it was because it was Saturday, but she didn't see either Mike or Randy, and she was able to have her boxes of screws rung up and bagged in record time. She made a mental note to shop at the hardware store on Saturday more often, and determinedly kept herself from scanning the sky. It was not going to rain.

Jaime drove straight to the house and parked in the driveway just as drops started to splatter her windshield.

"You said the rain had stopped!" she told her phone, and jumped out of the driver's seat. She pulled the plastic flagging off the back end of her pile of four-by-eight-foot sheets of plywood and yanked on the tie-down's rachet to loosen the load. Rain was starting to fall faster and faster.

She grabbed her work gloves and her carry rope from her tool bin. With an ease born from years of repetitive effort, she pulled the top piece of plywood toward her and leaned forward, slipping one end of the long rope loop around the far corner. She put the other end of the rope loop around the opposite corner and held the rope handle as she walked around to the far side of the plywood and slid the full sheet toward her. It was more awkward than heavy, but it was heavy enough to make her stagger a bit as its full weight transferred to her arms and shoulders.

She was going up the front steps, mostly sideways, wishing she could remember if there were four steps or five, when Mike Darden appeared with two to-go cups of coffee.

"Morning," he said, putting the coffee down on the edge of the porch. "Need a hand?"

It was just her luck that he would see her when she was struggling. She wanted to say she was fine, no problem, thanks for the offer, but the rain was starting to come down like it was never going to stop.

Jamie thumped the plywood onto the porch floor. She leaned it against the front of the house and made a quick decision. "Thanks. That would be great."

They hustled out to her truck and hauled the wood up to the porch, two sheets at a time. On the third and final trip, the rain started to come down in a serious way, and in unspoken accord, they trotted up the steps, reaching the covered porch just as heaven's floodgates opened wide.

"That was close," Mike said, laughing.

"Doesn't get much closer." Jaime grinned at him over the plywood. They placed the base of the last two sheets on the porch floor, up against the others, and moved toward each other to lean them up straight.

Their shoulders bumped. "Sorry," she murmured, glancing at him.

"No problem," he replied softly.

Jaime saw that his eyes were dark blue. His mouth was far closer to hers than she'd realized, and it seemed to be coming even closer. It had been a long time since she'd felt a man was attracted to her, and it felt good to have this particular man so close to her. She liked him. So why not go ahead and—

She suddenly remembered that she'd only kissed one other man in her life: Henry. What if she was horrible at it? What if she didn't know how to do it with anyone else? What if she'd learned bad habits? What if she kissed Mike and he walked away, wiping his mouth with the back of his hand? She wouldn't die of embarrassment, but she'd certainly want to, and she'd already filled her embarrassment quota for the decade, thank you very much.

With a jerk, she pulled away. "Thanks for your help," she said, her words coming out too fast. "I appreciate it."

"No problem," he said, stepping back. "Happy to."

"Well, um, thanks again."

"Sure." He paused. "You're welcome." After one more pause, he nodded, turned, and walked out into the pouring rain.

Jaime started after him, wanting to explain—it wasn't him, it was her, honest!—but fear held her back.

"You're a coward," she muttered to herself, and wondered how long it would take before she fully recovered from her marriage and divorce.

* * *

When the rain stopped, she used her ancient hand truck to carefully bump her brother's table saw out of her truck's cab and up the stairs to the primary bedroom. She ran timetables—and her desired level of personal comfort—in her head, and figured that in a week, she could move into the house herself.

The upstairs bathroom wasn't what you'd call modern, but the working essentials were there. And okay, there wasn't a functional kitchen, but she could borrow a small microwave oven from someone, and she was pretty sure she'd seen an old refrigerator in Demo's shed. If it worked, all she had to do was buy some beer and call a brother or two, and she'd have a bathroom and half a kitchen. What else did she need?

Sure, the building inspector might not agree, but there was no need to tell him every single little thing. She was always scrupulous about obtaining the proper permits. Was she doing anyone any harm by jumping the occupancy gun a teensy bit? She didn't see how.

The knowledge that she would soon have her very own living space made her smile, inside and out. "It'll be my first ever," she told Demo, who was supervising her efforts from a safe distance. She'd moved from the house where she'd grown up into the small house Arthur King had bought them for a wedding present, then a few years later to a bigger house, then to Lara's couch. "I've never lived alone before."

"Mmww," Demo said.

"Good point. I won't be alone, will I?"

"Mmww."

By now Jaime had resigned herself to the fact that Demo wasn't going anywhere. She needed to check with the animal shelter, but she had looked at the grocery store bulletin board and hadn't seen any sign of a flyer for a missing gray and white cat.

"If we're going to be living together," Jaime said, crouching down to fold out the saw's collapsible legs, "we should establish some ground rules. First, I don't eat your food and you don't eat mine. No wiggle room on that. Sleeping arrangements, we'll figure out as we go, and—"

She heard a quiet thump thump thump and turned just in time to see the tip of Demo's tail disappearing down the stairs. Of all the things she'd heard about cats, she'd never heard anyone ever say cat behavior had a marked resemblance to that of teenagers.

After that, the only time the rest of the morning she caught sight of Demo was through the window when she saw him trotting across the yard. Jaime figured that had more to do with the noise of the table saw than her attempt to discuss rules, but who knew with cats?

She went out to her truck at half past ten and grabbed the funeral service clothes she'd hung there last night. Back inside, she made sure all the sawdust was out of her hair and changed into a black sheath dress and slingback pumps, the only kind that didn't fall off her feet.

The Price's church was less than two miles away. Jaime arrived fifteen minutes before the service began, but the main parking lot was already full. She parked in the overflow lot and spotted her parents. Heels clicking, she hurried across the street to catch up. "I didn't know you two were coming," she said.

Her mother ran a head-to-toe gaze over her. She must have passed inspection, because her mom didn't make any comment on her appearance. "Of course we're here," she said. "Cilla was in my high school choir. And the Prices are in the community choir."

Jaime had forgotten both of those things. Since she'd been born with the musical ability of a toothbrush, details about the choirs her mom directed tended to get lost in the crooks and crannies of her memory.

Her dad straightened his tie and nodded. "Ladies?"

The three Moores climbed the steps to the church's front door, side by side, facing the horribly sad service as a family.

* * *

Afterward, Jaime stood in line with her parents to shake hands with Cilla's parents and siblings, everyone saying the sad, soft things you say. Once that was over, they went downstairs to the fellowship hall and got in line for the luncheon.

"Well, that was nice," her mom commented.

Jaime exchanged glances with her dad. Time for the post-service analysis.

"Sure was," her dad said.

Jaime caught sight of a face she hadn't expected to see. "Excuse me," she said to her parents. "Be right back."

She weaved through the crowd and touched the tall man on the elbow. "Detective Scoles," she said.

He turned. "Ms. Moore. I wondered if I'd see you here."

Jaime flicked a quick glance toward her parents. Not that it mattered if they saw her talking to a county sheriff detective, but it would better if they didn't see her talking to a county sheriff detective. Happily, luck was on her side, and her mom and dad were deep in conversation with the couple ahead of them in line.

She nodded at Scoles. "I was hoping to see you too."

He made a palms-up go-ahead gesture.

"I was wondering," Jaime said as quietly as she could, "if you'd been able to follow up with that woman, Ashley, that I called you about. Remember, she said she'd overheard Natalie Blake arguing with Cilla?"

The detective absently patted his suitcoat pocket, where Jaime could see the telltale flat bulge of a cell phone. "I've tried to contact her a number of times. Voicemail messages are not resulting in return calls."

Jaime managed not to roll her eyes, but it took a lot of effort. "Why haven't you sent her a text?"

He gave her a pained look. "Interview by the use of SMS is not an accepted law enforcement practice."

"Sure, but if it's the only thing you have?" Jaime could tell he wasn't buying it. "You could use a text to set up a day and time to call."

Sighing, he said, "Yes, that's the conclusion I've come to. Why is it, though, that some people find it so difficult to return a phone call?"

"I know what you mean," she said. There was a subcontractor she needed to talk to, but no matter what time she called, he never called back. If he didn't want the work, why didn't he just tell her? "Did you get my message about lumber kilns?"

"Yes, thank you," Detective Scoles said. "We're working on that. But I was going to call if I didn't see you at the service. I heard this morning from forensics. They've wrapped up at your house. You're free to work wherever you'd like."

A surge of glee washed through Jaime, and it was only an atavistic instinct for self-preservation that kept her from laughing out loud. Some things her mother would forgive, even many things, but laughter at a funeral luncheon before the food was gone was not one of them. "Thanks so much," she said, shaking the detective's hand, a wide smile stretching across her face. "That's great. I really appreciate that you told me right away. Thanks again."

She spun around, away from the amused expression on his face, and hurried over to her parents to make her excuses.

*   *   *

Fifteen minutes later, Jaime was back in her real clothes, tying her hair into a ponytail, settling a baseball cap on her head, and humming to herself. In a single instant, she'd gone from figuring out what she could productively do to having full control.

Well, as much control as you could have with any construction project. You were always at the mercy of other people's schedules, materials delivery, and the weather, but that was a given.

Jaime knew what had to happen first. The termite-infested basement floor joists had to be replaced. It was going to be expensive and time-consuming and noisy and messy, but that project was a priority. She could do demolition, make cabinets, and do all the planning she wanted, but until the structure was sound, it was insanity to do anything that even resembled final work. Right after that, she'd get her roofers on-site.

"Then electrical," she said. "And Plumbing. And HVAC." For days she'd been talking to her electrician friend, Glory, and her favorite plumber, Frank Gribbon, about scheduling, and now she could pull the trigger on specific days. But first things first. Now she could finally finish what she'd started a week ago.

She ran down the stairs, her spirits buoying her up so much that her work boots barely made a sound on the wood treads. The forensic people had made a massive mess of what she was desperately trying *not* to think of as Cilla's wall, and what she wanted more than anything was to finish knocking away the bits of cardboard from the ceiling and floor and to sweep it all away. Cilla needed to be remembered—certainly. But she needed to be celebrated for who she'd been and what she'd done, not for the way she'd died and not for where she'd been found.

Jaime found the push broom she'd left in the kitchen what seemed like months ago and approached the scatterings of plaster. She sent up a silent prayer for Cilla and got to work. But instead of thinking about what she'd get done between right then and when her floor joist guys, Tom and Jerry, showed up later that afternoon, she found herself thinking about murder suspects. And about lumber kilns.

She swept the pile of plaster dust into her long-handled dustpan and carried it into the kitchen. As she opened the back door, she heard Mike's distant voice. "Well, hey there, cat. How are you doing this afternoon?"

Carefully, quietly, she eased the door shut. She could take out the plaster dust later. After the man who'd almost kissed her was gone.

Chapter Eighteen

Jaime was embarrassed that she'd hidden from Mike. It had been an unexpected reflex, to back away and shut the door, but it had been one of those instinctive things. Of course, when people ignored their gut feelings in movies it always turned out badly, so maybe she shouldn't be embarrassed.

But why had she done it? He'd been two time zones away in Arizona when Cilla had been killed. He had nothing to do with Cilla's death. But . . .

Jaime sighed. But he'd been dating Cilla. And though he didn't seem to be grieving in any serious way, looks could be way deceiving. The last thing she needed was to be someone's rebound romance. What she did need was to find out, once and for all, who had murdered Cilla. She needed proof, not guesses and hypotheticals.

Unfortunately, guesses and hypotheticals were the primary contents of the suspect spreadsheet. She and Lara didn't have any proof of anyone doing anything, and slapping someone with suspicion of being a killer without any evidence was beyond irresponsible. Any taint of being a suspect could seriously damage someone's reputation, and Jaime didn't want to think about how hard it might be to recover from that kind of social media chatter. For her, the aftermath of That

Day had pushed her to go dark on social media for months. An accusation of a serious crime might make her deactivate all her accounts.

She finished cleaning up the cardboard and plaster dust and stood there. Had it really been only a week ago that she'd swung that sledgehammer? It hardly seemed possible. A week ago, she hadn't known Cilla was dead, let alone that the remains had been moved into her house.

Having access to the house was important, but shouldn't they also be asking who had even known the house was empty?

She blew out an annoyed breath, because there was no way of figuring that out. Almost anyone in town could have known. And anyone who knew the house was vacant could have known about the key, which had obviously been there a long time. She made a mental note to remember to look at the house's title work to see how many times it had changed hands in the last few decades. Maybe there'd be a clue in there.

Slightly cheered at the idea of investigative progress, she went upstairs to get some cleaning done before Tom and Jerry arrived. She took a quick inventory of the supplies she had on hand, then headed out for a quick trip to the closest dollar store.

Halfway there, she caught sight of a white panel van. It was parked in the driveway of a large monstrosity of a house. Jaime had driven by that house hundreds if not thousands of times in her life, and her opinion now was the same it had been from the get-go. It was the ugliest house in the universe.

Jaime slowed to take a look, and yes indeed, the guys in the black jeans and black T-shirts were wandering around, equipment in hand. She looked around and didn't see any sign of either a King Contractors truck or a yellow convertible.

She pulled to the curb and climbed out. "Hey," she said as she walked up the driveway. "You're the crew that's in town for a few days, right?"

Two of the guys glanced at the third, who was coiling up a length of cable. He nodded and came forward. "That's us. What can I do for you?"

"Satisfy my curiosity, mostly." The guy looked about ten years older than she was but had that look that came from spending a lot of time outdoors without wearing a hat or sunscreen.

Mr. Too Much Sun didn't say anything, so Jaime went on. "I thought you were doing something for the Chamber of Commerce, but the Chamber said no. And now I've seen you with Henry King and Natalie Blake. I suppose I could ask either one of them"—if there was no one else left on the planet—"but I was driving past and saw you, so . . ." She shrugged, smiling.

The guy smiled back. "We're working on a pilot for a television show. One of those home renovation things."

With everything she'd known, she should have seen that coming, but she hadn't. After a shocked moment, she asked, "Really? I would have thought the market for those was pretty saturated."

"You'd think," the guy said, shaking his head. "But what's one more, right? The thing that makes this one a little different is that Henry and Natalie are a young couple just starting their business, and they came up with this great idea to choose a theme song for every house. The final song choice is part of the end reveal."

Jaime didn't know what part of that infuriated her more, the "just starting their business" part or the "they came up with this great idea" part. She pasted on a smile. "No kidding. I had no idea Henry and Natalie were interested in television work."

"From what Henry said, he's wanted to do this for a long time, but he was married to someone who was holding him back. Now that he's divorced, he's free to follow his dream of having his own show."

"Holding him back," she repeated.

"Yeah," the guy said. "Sounds like the ex-wife wasn't TV material at all."

"Interesting." Jaime tried to smile through her gritted teeth but didn't do a very good job. She thanked him and stalked back to her vehicle, fury filling every cubic inch of her.

She'd been the one holding *him* back? *Seriously?*

* * *

By the time Jaime got to the dollar store, she'd cooled down enough to feel pretty sure that she wouldn't bite the head off everyone who came within ten feet of her.

She opened the truck's door, then shut it again. The film crew guy in black had mentioned the name of the network doing the pilot. Not that she could remember it, but she was sure if she saw it again, she'd recognize the name.

Tapping her phone back to life, she opened the LinkedIn app and entered Cilla's name. She'd meant to look this up the other night, but it had slipped her mind.

"Ahh . . ." she murmured, looking at her phone's screen. Cilla did have a profile on LinkedIn. It did list the network she'd worked for out in California, and it was indeed the same network that the guy in black said he was working for.

It was a huge connection between Cilla and Henry and Natalie. But did it have anything to do with Cilla's murder?

Jaime slid her phone back into her pocket and went into the store. Should she tell Detective Scoles what she'd learned? Practically every time she'd passed on some information, he'd already known it, so odds were good that he was already aware of the network connection, and Jaime was late to the investigative party. Not that she'd ever been invited.

She toyed with that thought as she added three jugs of general cleaner to her cart. Never once in her life had she crashed a party or gone where she wasn't wanted. Maybe it was time for that to change.

Why should she let someone else—anyone else—dictate what she did and where she went?

"Take both," a voice at her back said. "It's hard to have too many."

Jaime jumped. She'd been staring, unseeing, at the store's narrow selection of mops and hadn't registered that an employee was walking behind her. "Um, thanks," she said, but the woman was already gone.

The notion stuck with her, though, as a cashier tallied up her purchases. She tried not to flinch at the total and handed over her credit card with a sigh.

"Hard to have too many," the clerk had said. And some people never had enough, no matter what. Some people were just plain greedy.

She pushed her purchases outside and loaded them into her vehicle, still thinking.

In her head, she reviewed the column in Lara's spreadsheet titled "Motive." She highlighted the column in her mental spreadsheet and thought about the remaining suspects. Were they greedy?

Henry and Natalie? Absolutely yes.

Warren Brookshire? No idea.

Roger?

She shied away from the last one and tapped her fingers on the steering wheel, thinking about her one degree of separation from Brookshire. Ann Marie Dawkins, her favorite former client, had told her a fair amount about the man, none of it good. Would she be willing to ask Ann Marie more pointed questions about him? And what could possibly justify Jaime asking?

There was only one real answer to that.

Before she could change her mind, she opened her phone and called Ann Marie.

"Jaime!" she said. "Twice inside a week? To what do I owe the pleasure?"

The real answer was the truth. So she told Ann Marie about how she'd wanted to help the police find the murderer, for her own sake, so she could get back inside the house as soon as possible, but that it had shifted more to finding justice for Cilla. "Plus," Jaime said uncomfortably, because she was about to lay herself open, "I keep thinking that finding out who murdered Cilla will let her rest easier."

There was a long moment of silence. Jaime waited for a muffled snort of laughter. But it never came.

"Okay," Ann Marie said. "I'm on board. How can I help?"

Jaime's neck muscles loosened. "Great. Thanks. What I want to know is more about Warren Brookshire."

"Warren?" Her voice went high. "You think he's the one who—"

"Right now I'm just looking at possibilities," Jaime cut in. The last thing she wanted was for Ann Marie to start staring daggers at her boss, alerting him that something was up and possibly getting herself fired. "If he and Cilla hadn't gotten along, if they'd had an argument, that could be important."

Ann Marie made a snorting noise. "Warren doesn't get along with anyone. But I can tell you what the rumor mill is saying, that he's pushing for a big promotion with corporate and for a huge signing bonus. The chief executive position at our parent company's largest subsidiary—it's out in Colorado—is opening up. Dollars to doughnuts that's the job Warren wants."

And, Jaime realized, that was probably why he wanted to sell his share of the Corner Bar and Grill. Nothing nefarious there—just good business sense.

Though they talked for a few more minutes, Ann Marie didn't have anything more to add. Jaime thanked her for her time and asked that if she thought of something else, to give her a call.

When Jaime hung up, she realized she had new and even bigger questions.

Why exactly was Warren Brookshire trying to leave Green River? Was it because he was ambitious and taking a new opportunity? Or was it because he'd murdered Cilla Price and wanted to get far, far away?

*   *   *

Jaime hauled her new cleaning supplies into the house and went to work. Back in the day, she and whatever crew members were handy would do the cleaning. She'd never minded the task, although it was faster when she had two or three guys working along with her.

She was also discovering that working by herself instead of with crews that always had multiple radios blaring meant she had a lot of time to think. More time than she could ever remember having. If all went according to the business plan she was starting to form, she'd have her own crew again soon, so she told herself to stop feeling lonely and instead focus on the rare opportunity being offered her: time to herself.

Right now, she should be using that thinking time to work out what she'd learned so far about murder suspects. About their personalities. About motives. "And alibis," she said out loud. The spreadsheet column for alibis was basically empty, if she recalled correctly.

"Mmww!"

She clued into the fact that water was dripping from the sponge she was using to clean the bathroom ceiling, down her arm and off her elbow, dropping past the ladder she was perched on, and onto the floor.

And apparently onto a gray and white cat.

Jaime looked down and received a look that could kill from Demo. "Well, sorry, but how am I supposed to know you're down there if you don't let me know?"

"Mmww."

"To clarify, what you're telling me is that when I do anything ever, I should first check to make sure it's okay with you?"

"Mmww!"

"Got it." She wondered if cats understood sarcasm—because if any species outside of humans grasped the concept, it had to be cats.

Since she'd never thought Lara's theory that a good spreadsheet could solve everything had any factual basis, she hadn't paid much attention to the development of this particular version. Belatedly, she was seeing its virtues and almost wished she'd taken Lara up on her offer to put the file into a shared drive so they could both see it.

Almost, but not quite.

She climbed down the ladder, moved it six feet over, and climbed back up. After rinsing her sponge in the bucket hanging from the ladder's paint can hook, she glanced around for Demo, and seeing nothing but worn linoleum, reached up again.

Alibis. Was there any way for her to figure out who had one? It's not like she could call Henry and ask him what he was doing on the night of March 16.

Okay, technically she could, but she wasn't going to. And even if she did, he'd ask why she wanted to know, and she wouldn't have a good reason. Besides, he could always just lie about it. Same thing with Natalie, Warren Brookshire, and Mike Darden. Not that she really suspected Mike, because he had no real motive, but she didn't want to not consider him, just because she . . . well, because she liked him.

If she came up with a vague reason that Roger might buy into, he'd just say he was at the poker game that night. Which was true. And she wasn't sure she could conjure up a casual way to ask about a specific time frame, not for something that happened more than a month earlier.

"Well, duh."

She said the words at the ceiling and they echoed straight back into her face.

There was one way she could check on Henry and Natalie. She'd bet Natalie's privacy settings were wide open, and she knew for a fact that Natalie posted photos of practically every meal she ate and every drink she ordered.

With the ceiling done, she clambered down, pulled her cell phone from her pocket, and sat on a ladder rung. She scrolled through Natalie's posts on Facebook, going backward in time through April and into March. And there, on March 16, was a selfie of Henry and Natalie, cheek to cheek. They were at a restaurant table full of people Jaime assumed were Natalie's friends, because they looked ten years younger than Henry. Time posted was half past nine, and she'd written "Me and Henry on a Thursday night, out on the town in Charlotte."

Jaime squinted at her phone. The post was sort of an alibi, but not a complete one. Because the photo could be from a different night, even though she'd posted it on the 16th. Or if he'd left right after she'd posted the photo, and done a little speeding, he could have found Cilla at the airport at the right time.

Sighing, she typed in "Warren Brookshire" and then "Roger Goodwin." She checked each person associated with the names, but none who showed up matched the ones living in Green River.

"This investigating thing is harder than it looks," she muttered.

Because even though she didn't want to think about Roger committing murder—had actively avoided considering it although she knew that would have been the responsible thing to do—she still couldn't eliminate her dad's best friend as a suspect.

Chapter Nineteen

The cleaning went about as Jaime had expected. Slowly. On the plus side, doing every inch of it by herself and by hand meant that she saw everything up close and personal. As she wiped down the ceiling, she decided that the existing crown molding, the trim where the wall and ceiling met, was in good enough shape to stay. The plaster walls needed some serious patching, but not replacing. All of it would need repainting, but that was expected.

She turned around in the spacious bathroom, mentally repainting and replacing fixtures and flooring.

Ceiling? Soft white. The trim and the cabinets she was making? Bright white. Walls? Robin's egg blue. Fixtures? Faucets of brushed nickel with white porcelain. The claw-foot tub was in good enough shape to be resurfaced, but she'd have it moved over to make room for a good-sized walk-in tile shower. Shower tiles? So many choices—and all expensive. The rectangular subway tiles were popular and cheaper, but a mosaic was starting to shimmer in her head. If she slept on it for a day or two, she was sure the vision would solidify into a real idea.

It was time to get serious.

She pulled out her phone, opened the folder she'd created for the project, and started a task list. At the top of the list was "Carpet and tile store," because what she was thinking about would take time. If she could convince Lyle at the store to save boxes of broken tiles for her, instead of throwing them away or spending his time trying to return them for a refund, she'd buy them for a fraction of full price. She didn't care what shape or size tiles—she'd take anything. Then she could lay them out and create . . . something.

Her phone rang, startling her so much she almost dropped it. She glanced at the screen and took the call. "Hey, Ann Marie. What's up?"

"Do you want all the gossip on Warren Brookshire?" her former client asked.

"Yes. What do you have?"

"Not me. His former assistant. He just fired her. We're about to go have a celebratory drink in that new place downtown. You in?"

Fifteen minutes later, Jaime had crossed the back downtown parking lot and was opening a wood door and climbing a flight of steps into River City Brewing. She looked around in the suddenly dim light and saw Ann Marie waving at her.

She felt the wood floor creak under her feet as she crossed the room. River City was all hard surfaces—wood floor, tin ceiling, brick walls—and any sound seemed to bounce around until it faded away completely. But in spite of the noise, Jaime enjoyed the place. The owner had found historical photos of the area, enlarged them, and mounted them on the walls. She especially liked the sepia-toned aerial view of downtown. Judging by the cars, it had been taken around 1920, back before the fire that had taken out Anderson's Department Store, and before the city had planted trees next to the curbs.

Ann Marie made the introductions, and Jaime sat down across from Felicia Tousely, who had shiny brown hair that cascaded down to the middle of her back

"Nice to meet you," she said, her accent indicating origins deeper in the South. "Ann Marie here says you're looking for dirt on that—"

She stopped and took a breath. "No, my mama always told me to speak kindly of those who do us harm."

Jaime slid Ann Marie a sidelong glance. If Felicia wasn't going to talk about Warren, this time was going to be wasted.

"No name-calling." Ann Marie nodded. "We understand."

"Good." Felica pushed a stray wisp of hair back behind her ear. "I'll tell the truth, the whole truth, and nothing but the truth."

Jaime looked at Anne Marie, who gestured at her to go ahead. "Thanks. I guess, first off, what was he like as a boss?"

"Horrible," Felicia said without hesitation. "Worst boss I've ever had. When my old boss retired, I knew it was going to be difficult, but Warren Brookshire was much harder to work for than I could have imagined."

"Micromanager?" Jaime suggested.

"Top to bottom, inside and out." Felicia picked up her pint glass and took a long swallow. "Which was bad enough, but he's also inconsistent in how he wants things done. And don't get me started on how unrealistic his expectations are."

Once again, Jaime patted herself on the back for her career choices. "Have there been any recent changes in his behavior?"

"Not for the better."

Jaime and Ann Marie laughed, and Felicia quirked up a small smile. "You know, Ann Marie here didn't say why ya'll are looking for information on Warren."

"It's about Cilla Price," Jaime said. Luckily, she'd prepped herself for this question on the drive over. "I knew her in high school, and since I'm the one who found her body, I feel some responsibility. I want to make sure she rests easy. If Warren treated her badly, I'll do what I can to make sure he's held accountable."

Felica's smile widened. "I like the sound of that. Recent changes? He's been pushing everyone hard to finish the speed testing for a new chip ahead of schedule. That way they move up the rollout and get production numbers higher than the projections. But don't ask me why this year is more important than any other year. Executive assistants aren't told things like that."

The conclusion, Jaime felt, was that Warren was under a lot of pressure. Interesting. Jaime was starting to thank her for her time when Felicia held up an index finger.

"Hobbies, though. There was one thing. He was really into woodworking."

The thunderbolt knowledge of Warren Brookshire's woodworking expertise silenced Jaime.

She was never at her best in group situations, and during awkward ones her typical reaction had been to retreat and let Henry deal with it. But there was no Henry. And she needed to figure out how to work through social discomfort all on her own. Starting right then and there.

She coughed, clearing her clear throat, and took a drink of the light ale that had appeared in front of her. "Sorry," she murmured. "Woodworking, you said?"

Felicia nodded. "That's right. He was forever talking about jigs and clamps and glue. Because I was a good assistant, I listened and pretended to care, but did he ever let me talk about my rose garden?" She made a face. "If I got more than one sentence in, it'd be because he wasn't listening in the first place."

"I used to have a husband like that," Jaime said absently, and was surprised when Ann Marie snorted with laughter. "Anyway," Jamie went on, half smiling, "is there anything else you can tell me about him?"

"His family life is what you'd expect." Felicia held up two fingers. "Couple of kids. Divorced. His ex-wife and daughters live in Virginia. He leaves early every other Friday to get the girls and comes in late the following Monday."

Marginally interesting, but since Cilla had disappeared on a Thursday, Jaime didn't see how that could be relevant. What would be extremely relevant was whether or not Brookshire had a lumber kiln. Smiling, she tried to drag the conversation in that direction. "I'm a woodworker myself," she said, "so I get the tool thing. But I thought divorced guys had apartments or condos. Most of them don't have much room for a good-sized shop."

"He lives in an old farmhouse out on Wiley Road, the other side of the interstate," Felicia said. "A couple of times he had me take packages out there. The house isn't that big, but there were barns. His shop is probably in one of them."

"Wiley Road." Jaime nodded. "I renovated a house out there about five years ago. Big yellow one. Is Brookshire's house near it?"

"You did that house? It's gorgeous." Felicia smiled. "His place is maybe a mile past that. Past that little crick."

And just like that, Jaime knew what her next step was going to be.

*   *   *

The next morning, she left the apartment long before most people's alarms went off. She drove out to Wiley Road, averting her eyes as she drove past the yellow house, which was festooned with more gingerbread trim than should exist on five houses. The owners had loved it, but Jaime couldn't look at the place without thinking about how much work it would be to repaint. She'd tried many times to convince them to go with PVC instead of wood, and every time the husband had wrinkled his nose and said, "No plastic on my house."

At the last second, she stole a quick glance and laughed out loud, because even in the dim light of early dawn, she could see painter's scaffolding all across the front of the house.

Still smiling, she drove over the interstate and slowed as she crossed Landis Creek. She slowed even more as she came near a white farmhouse. Lights were on both upstairs and down, so she kept driving. A mile down the road, empty of traffic at six in the morning, she did a quick three-point turn and went back the way she'd come.

The lights in the farmhouse hadn't changed. She drove to the creek, where there was a packed earth parking lot made from years and years of people pulling off the road to park and fish. She backed deep into a grove of birch trees, rolled her windows down, turned off her truck's engine, and waited.

From the bullying episode at the gas station, she knew that Brookshire owned an old Ford Mustang, and Felicia had told her that he'd recently bought the black Ford Expedition Jaime had seen in the CS parking lot. "One of those fancy Platinum models," she'd said. "After he bragged about how much it cost, I said that much money could have been the tipping point for curing cancer." She'd smiled. "That might have been when he decided he needed to fire me."

Jaime, her back to the rising sun, saw the dawn in her rearview mirror, listened to the birds, and watched the road. A very long half hour later, a great big black Ford SUV went by. She waited ten minutes, then pulled out and went to Brookshire's house, turning around in the driveway so she could make a quick exit.

Not that she'd need to, of course. But it didn't hurt to be prepared.

She got out and looked around. From here, she couldn't see a single neighbor. Convenient, if you were the murdering type. She could see half a dozen old outbuildings of various ages and sizes, but she didn't care so much about them. A lumber kiln, with all that heat, was sure to be outside in its own dedicated structure.

Jaime grabbed her disguise from the back seat—a clipboard—and started on a quick self-guided tour of Brookshire's property.

She made circuits around the house, a hay barn, an old tobacco barn, a tractor shed, and a long, low outbuilding that had likely been a stable not that long ago. There was an old truck in the shed, a pile of scrap metal heaped behind the tobacco barn, and a stack of tarped rough-sawn hardwood next to the shop.

But no lumber kiln.

Chapter Twenty

When Jaime arrived at the house, ready for a long day of work, she was greeted by a purring cat as soon as she shut the door of her truck. She looked down into Demo's golden-brown eyes and suddenly felt compelled to tell him the truth about her trip to Warren Brookshire's house.

"I really thought it was him," she said, crouching down to pet the cat, who'd flopped onto the grass and was rolling belly up. "I was so sure. I just *knew* I'd find a lumber kiln on his property."

The whole thing was embarrassing. And she certainly wouldn't ever tell anyone, not even the cat, that she'd walked around Brookshire's property with her cell phone on, her contacts list open, and her thumb poised to push the button for calling Detective Scoles.

Demo's ears swiveled, and he bolted pell-mell across the yard, in the direction of his shed.

Half a second later, Mike Darden pushed through the lilacs. "Morning, neighbor!"

Jaime could see that once again he was bringing her a mug of coffee. But this time she had something to give him in return.

"Take one." She held out the box of apple fritters she'd picked up at the Chestnut Street Bakery as she'd come back through town. She'd called ahead and Tracy had had it ready and waiting for her. "They're still warm, but my floor joist crew is due to arrive soon, and those guys eat like there's no such thing as cholesterol. Or calories."

"Whoa," Mike said, peering in. "Each one of these would feed a family."

Jaime laughed. "I've often thought the same thing." She waited a beat, then sallied forth. "Um, I'm sorry about the other day. Sending you out into the rain like that. I didn't mean to . . . I mean . . . um . . ."

Mike chose the fritter closest to him. "No worries. I didn't melt."

He looked up at her, and his smile was so warm and inviting that she leaned toward him. "I'm glad," she said.

"You are?" he asked.

"I absolutely am."

He nodded, still smiling. "Well. That's good to hear."

Before her common sense caught up with the rest of her, she asked the question that had been rattling around in her head for days. "Um, I hear you and Cilla Price had been seeing each other. Having her disappear like that, then finding out she was murdered? That has to be hard for you."

A crumble of apple fritter fell from Mike's hand onto the ground. He stared at her. "You heard what?"

Jaime's face started to heat up. "Maybe I got it wrong. But I thought heard you two had been . . . dating?"

He shook his head. "Only if you count as dating a couple of cups of coffee to get some advice on employee attraction and retention. Me? I'd think of it more as networking between two members of the Chamber of Commerce."

"Oh. Well. I guess someone jumped to the wrong conclusion." She made a vow that the next time she ran into Randy Johnston, she'd be sure to tell him so.

"Absolutely." Mike gave the house a searching glance. "But knowing that she was in there all those weeks when I was right next door? What I guess I feel is guilt, in a weird sort of way."

"There's nothing you could have done," Jaime said. "She was dead long before her body was put there."

The back of his hand brushed across hers, igniting a shivering spark that ran up her arm and straight to her heart.

"Thanks," Mike said quietly. "I appreciate that. But I still feel like I should have been able to do something."

Jaime knew exactly how he felt, because she felt the same way. She and Mike, it seemed, felt the same way about a lot of things. Maybe it was time for her to explore that. Maybe she was ready to—

The horns of two pickup trucks blared, signaling the arrival of Tom and Jerry, her floor joist guys. Five minutes later, the apple fritters and coffee were gone, and Mike had made his way back through the lilac bushes. Jaime watched him go, reliving their conversation, until Jerry bumped her elbow.

"Ready to rock and roll?" he asked, rubbing his meaty hands.

Tom, his business partner of thirty years, gave him a long, sad look. "We're going to spend the day in a snake-infested crawl space, and you're happy about it?"

"No snakes," Jaime said confidently, repeating the information she'd told Jerry the day before and that he had apparently not passed on to Tom. "No rats, no mice. No termites, no bugs. No critters of any kind." The exterminators had finished the week before, and she'd been happy to pay full price for the privilege. Way more than happy. Critters were fine in their place, but their place was outside the house, never in.

Part of the reason she'd been so happy had been because earlier, after Tom and Jerry had given the joists a thorough inspection, they'd given her the good news that the termite damage wasn't too horrible.

The weakened joists weren't the primary structural joists that kept the house from falling over, so the wood floors and subflooring on the main level wouldn't have to be pulled up after all.

Indeed, the only thing the weak joists supported was the flooring itself, which meant a fresh new joist could be installed right next to the old. *Sistering* it was called, and Jaime was looking forward to meeting the new siblings.

Tom nodded slowly. "No snakes. That does brighten my day. Jaime, ladies first, yes?" He held open an open palm, inviting her into the crawl space.

Though it had taken some talking to convince them to reduce their cost by the cost of her time spent on the job—and a demonstration of her ability to handle a pneumatic nail gun—the pleased expressions on their faces right then told her they'd warmed to the idea. It probably had more to do with the fact that their regular hired hand had turned in his tool belt for a computer, but whatever worked.

Jaime eased into the crawl space and squirmed around on her back until she found a spot that didn't have a rock poking into her spine. "Ready," she called out.

"You fit in there right easy, don't you?" Tom, his big body blocking most of the light from the hatchway, peered at her.

"It's not too bad," she said.

"Once the joists are moved, we'll get down there with you to glue and lift while you nail. Here comes the first one." He disappeared from view, and with a thump, the front end of the first joist hit the dirt next to her.

Jaime looked at the chunk of yellow pine, all two inches by twelve inches by twenty feet of it. The day was going to be a long one.

* * *

After the afternoon break for water and before their stomachs told them it was time to quit, the last joist was glued up, sistered, and nailed in place.

They crawled out into the sunlight, and all three turned their faces to the sun. "Now that's a good day's work," Jerry said. "Tell you what, Jaime. If you ever decide you want to come work for two guys on the edge of geezerdom, you give me a call."

Tom opened the cooler he'd put next to the house during afternoon break, and offered cans of beer all around. "Got that right," he said, popping his open. "Your little arms are small enough to fit in tighter places than we can get to without adding elbows where they don't belong. And you got enough stamina to go the day."

She wasn't sure he was super right about the stamina thing. Her body ached from top to bottom. "Thanks," she said, smiling, "but I prefer aboveground work."

They chatted companionably until the cans were empty. Then the men climbed into their pickups, with Jaime calling after them to send her an invoice, and they went their separate ways.

It had been a good day, Jaime thought as she started her pickup. She would sleep like a rock that night, which was a huge benefit of physical labor. Plus, it had all been done in less time than Tom and Jerry had estimated, and they'd said the invoice would reflect that.

She headed to Lara's apartment, but halfway there she thumped the steering wheel with her fist.

Demo. She'd been so wound up with the floor joists that she'd neglected to check on the cat's food and water supplies. Sighing, she turned around in a gas station driveway and headed back the way she'd come, back through Green River's downtown corridor.

Just past the post office but before the hardware store, she saw Natalie's friends, Ashley and—what had the other one's name been?

Brittany. She saw the two women walk out of a boutique shoe store, both of them carrying shopping bags.

She pulled over and braked to a hard stop at the curb. She had a question about Natalie, and there was no time like the present.

"Ashley?" she called, hopping out. "And Brittany, right? We met in the grocery store the other day."

"Oh yes, I remember." Ashley squinched up her nose. "You're the one who wanted me to talk to that detective. He kept leaving message after message. Finally, I took matters into my own hands and picked up the phone and called him myself."

"That's, uh . . . good." Jaime heard herself sound like Roger Goodwin and shook away the thought. "I had a quick question for you, if that's okay. You're good friends with Natalie, right? Do you have any idea if she met Henry King because of that TV show pilot they're working on?"

The two younger women exchanged glances. "You know about that?" Ashley asked. "I thought it was a secret."

Jaime smiled. "Green River is a small town. People talk."

"Oh. Well."

Ashley looked at Brittany. Brittany looked at Ashley. Neither one said anything.

"Okay, look," Jaime said, opting for the truth. "I'm asking because I'm Henry's ex-wife." She watched their faces register shock, then speculation. She shook her head. "Natalie is welcome to him, Scout's honor. Truly. But I'm curious about the timing of when they started seeing each other."

More glances were exchanged.

Jaime sighed. She did not have time for this. Well, maybe she had the time. What she didn't have was the patience. "I'm not out for revenge," she said. "I'm much happier without him than I was with him"—something she hadn't fully realized until that moment—"but there are things I need to understand if I'm ever going to get closure."

"Oh, sure," Ashley said. "If you put it that way. I get it."

"I don't remember exactly when they started seeing other?" Brittany moved closer. "But it was right after Natalie was on that morning news show. You know, that local one that does little stories of things going on in town? *Good Morning in Green River* I think it is?"

In the depths of her dreary divorce-induced days, Jaime had spent her TV time binge-watching *Grey's Anatomy* and *Heartland*, but she'd heard of the morning show, so she nodded.

"Well, Natalie was on . . . um, last fall?" Brittany looked at Ashley.

"Had to be," Ashley said. "Nat was here downtown, looking for a skirt to go with her new boots. This TV reporter talked to her right there on the sidewalk, asking about fashion trends."

"That's right," Brittany said. "And you know how Nat glows when she talks about clothes and shoes and hairstyles."

Jaime did not, but she said, "It was a good interview, then?"

"The best," Ashley said, beaming. "We watched the clip over and over again. And right after that is when Henry tracked her down and hired her to work for him. Told her that the camera loves her, and had she ever thought about going into television. Don't you think that's the sweetest thing ever to say?" She giggled.

Jaime did not. But she thanked the women and, driving away, tried to put all the pieces together. She was still in the assembly stage when she got to the house and went to the shed.

"So here I thought that I got divorced because Henry cheated on me," she said to Demo as she refilled the food and water bowls. "Okay, that's absolutely true, but Henry wanted to divorce me so he could host a TV show with a more suitable partner. That has to be one of the dumbest things I've ever heard."

She hitched herself up onto the seat of a rusty lawn tractor that looked as if it hadn't been started in fifty years. "Now I'm wondering what that means, motive-wise, for Cilla's murder."

"Mmww," a quiet voice said.

"Exactly." Jaime stopped "Almost from the beginning I was sort of trying to convince myself that Henry or Natalie, or Henry and Natalie, had murdered Cilla. But why would they?"

She thought back to all she'd learned in the last week and half. Henry had been talking to Cilla about her network contacts. Natalie had been angry at Cilla for not getting a job she'd wanted. If either one of them had been psychopaths, sure, that might have tipped them over the edge. But just because they were pathetic excuses for human beings didn't mean they were killers.

"I don't think either one of them murdered Cilla," she said. "That leaves two people." She displayed the requisite number of fingers to Demo. "Warren Brookshire and my dad's best friend."

"Mmww?"

"Brookshire seems nasty enough, but I still haven't found a reason for him to murder Cilla. Roger, though. If Cilla was trashing his reputation online, there's motive right there."

She loved Roger. He had the kindest heart of anyone she'd ever met As a kid, she'd given him atrocious gifts she made in her dad's shop, and he'd loved them all. She couldn't imagine him as a killer. He just couldn't be.

But she was very afraid that he was.

*   *   *

Jaime spent most of that night staring at the ceiling, thinking through everything she'd learned since the day she'd swung her sledgehammer against a wall that shouldn't have existed. In the morning, Lara having spent the night at her fiancé's place, Jaime took a long, hot shower, followed by a ten-second burst of cold water.

It was a technique her mom had taught her years earlier—*"Some mornings it takes more than coffee"*—and every so often she admitted that her mom knew her pretty well. She didn't like to admit it out loud, but it didn't hurt to give a general thank-you, so she did. "Thanks, Mom," she said softly.

A bowl of cereal and a travel mug full of coffee later, she headed to her first stop of the day, Beason Lumber. Right afterward, she was going to do what she should have done days ago, swing past Roger's office again and corner Donna Neely, Roger's office manager. There had to be a way to learn more about Roger. To figure out once and for all if Cilla had been a threat to his practice. To prove his innocence or . . . or not.

If she couldn't learn anything from Donna, she'd try Ann Marie again. Maybe someone else at CS had been fired by Warren Brookshire. Maybe that someone would be willing to talk to her, and just maybe that someone would provide a bit of critical information.

She pulled into the loading area of Beason Lumber and hopped out. Sami Beason was on the other side of the yard, huddled with a trio of employees, a clipboard in hand and a serious look on her face. Doug Beason was nearby, chatting with a man about his own age.

"Hey, Doug," she said into a conversational lull between the two.

"Morning, Jaime," he said. "You know Mason Price? Mason, Jaime Moore—Brad and Stephany's youngest."

Jaime was suddenly and acutely aware that she was face to face with Cilla's father. "Mr. Price. That was a . . . a nice service on Tuesday."

"You were there?" The gray-haired man shook his head. "Right. Of course you were. You were the one who . . . well. Thank you for coming to the service. We appreciate that so many of Cilla's friends were there."

An awkward silence fell hard. Jaime scratched around in her brain for something to say. "Um, I hear Cilla was well liked at CS. Everyone I know there speaks highly of her." All two of them.

Mason's gaze, which had been wandering, suddenly sharpened. "Do they? I appreciate the sentiment, but you're not talking about her boss, are you?"

Now Jaime's attention was caught. "No," she said. "I hear he's a piece of work."

Mason snorted. "Cilla couldn't stand the man. She was looking for another job."

"Oh? Because he was a such a bully?"

"That, and something about fake speeding." He shrugged. "I didn't understand it myself. All that tech stuff is way above my head."

A thought snagged in Jaime's head. Something about speeding. Or was it just speed? No, a something kind of speed . . . car speed? Project speed? No, no, and no.

And then she remembered. Felicia had talked about chip speed. She'd said Brookshire had been pushing hard to finish the speed testing for a new semiconductor chip, that he wanted production numbers higher than projections.

She finished the conversation with Cilla's father, then backed away, pulled out her phone, and started texting Ann Marie.

Jaime: *Question. Does Warren Brookshire's promotion hinge on the results of the speed tests for those new chips?*

Ann Marie: *Yup.*
Jaime: *Can speed tests be faked?*
Ann Marie: *Nope.*
Jaime: *Could a report of the test results be faked?*
Ann Marie: *I suppose. Why?*
Jaime: *Will tell you later. Thanks.*

She slid her phone back into her pocket and edged back to the two men. "Mr. Price, one more thing. Do you know if Cilla had plans to do anything about her boss other than just quit?" As in, was she going to report up the corporate chain? Was she going to jeopardize his promotion? His career? His livelihood? His self-respect?

Mr. Price frowned. "About the faking? I'm not sure. But Cilla being Cilla, it wouldn't surprise me. She couldn't abide lies. If Brookshire was doing something wrong, she'd do her best to stop it."

"Brookshire?" Doug's bushy eyebrows went up. "Has a place out on Cruchley Road? We run deliveries out there maybe once a month. Plywood, mostly. Some drywall."

Jaime shook her head. "Must be a different Brookshire. Warren lives on Wiley Road."

"No, that's him," Doug insisted. "I mean, there can't be two Warren Brookshires in Perkins County, can there? He has a fantastic workshop. Every tool you can imagine except a kitchen—" Doug laughed. "No, I take that back. He has a kitchen sink out there too."

Jaime stared. No wonder she hadn't seen signs of a big shop at his house. Warren owned two properties, something that hadn't occurred to her. But the big question was, did the shop property have a lumber kiln?

There was only one way to find out.

Chapter Twenty-One

Cruchley was a narrow, twisting, turning road whose asphalt had seen its heyday before Jaime was born. She knew the road mainly because it was a shortcut to Charlotte, but because of the potholes, hardly anyone went that way unless they lived there.

The land out that way was mostly unpopulated swamp and farmland, which meant the traffic was nonexistent as she drove to Warren's property. Doug had given away the property's location after she'd vaguely mentioned a big barn on Cruchley just this side of the reservoir turnoff, saying that must be Brookshire's. "No," he'd said. "Brookshire's place is the same side of the road, but maybe two miles past that. Big white place you can hardly see from the road."

Jaime passed the reservoir turnoff, watching the odometer tick off with one eye and keeping the other eye out for a big white place.

It took her a while—she drove too far, turned around, came back, drove too far again, turned around again, rinse and repeat—but when she stopped searching for a white building and started looking for a narrow driveway, she found the place.

Or at least she thought it was the right place. While still on the broken Cruchley asphalt, she studied two thin tracks that led into the deep, dark woods; tracks that, if they could talk, would be able to tell her if they led to a place for a guy who just wanted to spend time alone, making projects out of wood, or if they led to the lair of a killer, which was probably creepily covered with kudzu vines.

"The shop is white," she said out loud. If Doug said the building was white, it couldn't be a creepy kudzu kind of place.

She tapped her pocket, making sure her phone was in place, and tried not to think that she could be basing her personal safety on the recollections of a semiretired man in his mid-sixties who couldn't reliably remember what day it was. Then again, she often used her phone to tell the day of the week, so who was she to throw judgmental stones?

Today, though, she knew Warren was at work, and this was her last good chance until Monday to search the property.

"Just looking around," she said to herself, getting her story straight, should the need arise. "Need a workshop myself, and I heard you might be moving on. Do you have a price?"

It wasn't a bad story, and it gave her the nudge she needed to take her foot off the brake and onto the gas pedal.

The driveway was rutted and bumpy enough to knock her fillings loose, but as she drove around a curve and up a small hill, it smoothed into minor ruts that barely rattled her dashboard. One more curve and then she saw what was undoubtedly a woodworking shop. There were stacks of raw lumber at both ends, stickered with smaller bits of wood to keep the faces from touching, and a dust collector standing tall and proud at the building's end.

Clearly visible through the plate glass windows that made up one full wall of the building was the biggest array of woodworking machines and tools Jaime had ever seen outside of a sales floor.

She got out of her truck and looked through the windows to what, as far as she was concerned, was prettier than the best Christmas window ever.

There was a table saw, a radial arm saw, and a lathe. A massive planer; a bandsaw; and not one, but two router tables. Brookshire had a sanding table, a mortising machine, an entire freaking wall of clamps—and it went on and on.

She took a deep breath and looked away, stamping down on the shop envy that was rearing its ugly head. Later. She could be jealous about Brookshire's shop later. Right now, she was here to find a lumber kiln.

If there was one here, it shouldn't be hard to find. She'd done enough research to know two things. It would be outside and it would be big. Plus, now that she knew Warren Brookshire was a tool hound, if he had a kiln it would probably be far larger than he needed.

She looked at her truck, parked out front like it had an appointment, like it belonged there. After a moment's thought, she climbed back in and moved the truck off to the side, so far back under a large poplar tree that her rear bumper tapped the tree's trunk. Not hiding, just taking advantage of the shade.

She tucked her pant legs into her socks, aware of the ticks and of a far-off traffic rumble, and pushed her way into the tall grass, half her attention near her feet to watch for snakes and other critters; the other half in front of her, looking for a lumber kiln.

To the left of Warren's shop, it was all grass and small trees so thick she couldn't see through. She sidled her way in, between the side of the shop and the scrubby branches, breathing a happy sigh of relief that none of them had thorns.

The scrub trees petered out as she went, and when she reached the shop's back corner, they'd given way to a clearing as wide as the shop itself. The clearing was shaded by a massive oak tree and dominated by an oddly shaped metal building. It was long enough to fit a good-sized boat, half that deep, and taller than the average garage.

A lumber kiln.

* * *

Jaime stared at the kiln long enough that her eyes started to dry out. Then she realized that her mouth had dropped open and it was dry too.

Blinking and swallowing, she inched her way forward.

Warren Brookshire had a lumber kiln. A kiln way more than big enough to hold a human body.

Warren Brookshire was a bully. She'd seen proof of that herself when he'd bullied that poor teenager at the tiniest hint of a provocation when he thought she might possibly have incurred a minute scratch on his antique car.

If Warren Brookshire wanted something, he wanted the best. Proof of that was in the shop. No hobbyist needed a shop anywhere near that large or with anywhere near that number of tools.

Warren Brookshire was ambitious, given what Ann Marie had said about him pushing for a promotion.

Add all that together, then add in his worst nightmare: someone who found out that he was faking test results, an HR director who knew right from wrong and had a long record of helping the underdog.

"He killed her," Jaime said quietly, and took out her phone.

Hardly any signal, of course. She stared at the single small rectangle of white, willing it to expand into a full set of bars. When it didn't, she took a photo of the kiln and sent it to Detective Scoles anyway, along with a text message: *Lumber kiln at Warren Brookshire's property on Cruchley Road. I think he murdered Cilla Price.*

Jaime hit "Send" and waited. It didn't bounce back as undeliverable, but there were no telltale dots of a response being typed either. She walked closer to the kiln, holding the phone up toward the sky, as if those three feet would make all the difference, but still got the same stubborn teeny tiny bar.

She wondered what Brookshire did for connectivity. There was no way a tech guy like him could live without the internet for long periods of time. Satellite access? Just barely, she kept herself from glancing up at the sky to look for one. Didn't matter. Whatever he had for Wi-Fi, it was certainly password protected.

Jaime stopped, her attention completely focused on the metal-sided kiln, now just an arm's length away. She didn't see any indication of lumber being dried, but she cautiously held out a hand to gauge its heat level.

Nothing.

Carefully, she put her hand on the smooth metal. Cool to the touch.

Huh. Somehow she'd expected it to be hot. Silly of her, she supposed. No reason for it to be, really, because of the thick insulation it needed to have. She tried to remember the temperatures home lumber kilns ran up to. Well over a hundred degrees, if she recalled correctly. Maybe two hundred? The number made her shiver. At least Cilla had been dead before she'd been put inside.

Her skin crawled with the creepiness of it all. She stepped backward, and her focus widened to take in more of the world around the kiln. A world that suddenly included the sound of an approaching vehicle.

Someone was driving up the hill.

There were only a handful of people it could be. A truck from Beason's with a load of plywood to drop off. Some other delivery truck. Or it could be Warren Brookshire, although he shouldn't be here. He should be at his desk on a Friday morning. He should be working hard, proving himself, trying to get that promotion.

If it was a delivery truck, she was fine. She could stay right where she was, and the truck would go back down the driveway, and the driver would never know she'd been there.

But if it was Warren Brookshire . . .

She looked at the expanse of windows that filled the back wall of the shop and felt naked.

The vehicle came to a stop. A door opened. "Hello?" a male voice called out.

Brookshire.

He must have seen her truck. He couldn't catch her there. He couldn't know she'd even been here. If he didn't see her, he'd have to assume someone left the truck there by mistake. Or abandoned it. He'd look around, shrug, and call to get it towed.

As long as he didn't find her.

Jaime thought it all through in the space of a heartbeat and made her decision.

Carefully, quietly, she unlatched one of the kiln's double doors, thick and heavy with heatproofing and insulation, and slipped inside. She pulled the door closed, but not shut all the way, leaving herself a small sliver of sunlight to peer through.

She waited.

Listened.

Waited and listened some more.

Just when she was sure Brookshire must have left without her hearing the car, she saw him inside the shop, striding from one end to the other, head turning this way and that.

Searching.

For her.

She pulled the door closer toward her, narrowing her field of view to nearly nothing. She desperately wanted to stop breathing, for her heart to stop beating, because she was sure their combined sound was loud enough to hear in Asheville. Just for a minute, of course—just long enough for Brookshire to realize that no one was there and to leave.

A door slammed.

Jaime let out a long breath. This was it. He'd looked through the shop and see that no one was there, nothing had been stolen. He'd get back in his Ford Expedition and—

Solid footsteps came closer and closer.

She held her breath. It was far too late to inch the door closed. He'd see the movement and know someone was inside. She looked for a place to hide, but there was nothing. She was inside a big rectangular metal box. There was stickered wood filling most of it, and there was metal equipment halfway down. There was absolutely nowhere to go.

But she could make up a story. He'd open the door, accuse her of trespassing, and she'd say she'd been . . . she'd heard about his wonderful shop. Sure, that was it. And then she got curious about the kiln, and wow, she was sorry to have trespassed, but what a great setup he had, and—

Slam!

Jaime staggered backward. Brookshire had shut the door in her face. She heard a clattering noise, the unmistakable sound of the door's heavy latch thudding into place.

And then he turned the kiln on.

Chapter
Twenty-Two

Jaime didn't know that he'd turned it on, not right away. At first she was too busy listening, trying to hear if he was still there or if he'd left. But with the door fully closed—and locked—the kiln's thick walls kept her from hearing anything except the sound of her own breaths going in and out at a rate far faster than usual.

She recognized she was having what had to be a normal reaction when shut in a small, dark space against your will. Scared? Of course she was scared. Anyone with the sense of a staple would be afraid. The trick was to control the fear. To not let it control her. There would be a way out of there. There had to be. All she had to do was find it.

The silent and private pep talk made her feel better. A few deep breaths and she'd be calm enough to start working on her escape route.

It was on inhale of the second intake of air that she registered a new sound. A humming, ticking sort of noise. The building wasn't fully airtight; some air and light filtered in through an exhaust fan near the ceiling. She could see that the blades of the vent weren't moving. When the kiln was running, they'd be whirling away, keeping the air flowing. So what was that noise?

Jaime pulled out her phone. She'd had a tiny shred of hope that the metal building might magically act as a signal amplifier and she'd have full bars. Her hope, sadly, was crushed. Science was still a thing, and the phone's screen announced the dreaded "No signal" message. But through sheer habit, she'd topped off the phone's charge in the truck on the way over, so at least there was that.

She tapped on the flashlight function and explored her small universe. A gauge near the door. Lumber down the right side. A narrow aisle all the way down to allow access to the lumber. Halfway down the aisle, the kiln itself, and the dehumidifier.

And that was it. No windows, no other exit, no nothing.

"Not even a stool to sit on."

She froze. Her voice had sounded way louder than she'd thought it would. What if Brookshire heard her?

Jaime rolled her eyes at herself and blew out a breath. So what if he did? He knew someone was in there. Why else would he have locked the door? Whether or not he knew it was Jaime Moore inside didn't really matter.

She clutched her useless communication device and tried to think, tried not to panic, tried not to scream for someone to come please get her out, tried to be adult and calm and resourceful.

But she was hot. And thirsty. And she was learning that it was hard for her to be resourceful while sweating bullets with a parched throat.

Lifting the T-shirt from her skin, she gave it a few flaps. Maybe she was imagining things. Maybe it was the fear that was making her sweat—maybe it wasn't the heat at all.

She walked over to the gauge next to the door and aimed the phone's light.

Wait, what?

Jaime stared. It was a simple temperature gauge. Not a digital readout, but an old-fashioned needle. The gauge's numbers ranged from eighty degrees to two hundred. The needle itself was buried deep into the nineties, close to one hundred.

Tick.

She whirled. The noise she'd been hearing. She hadn't been paying much attention to it, because lumber kilns were loud. They had to be. Vents and fans circulated the air constantly, and vents and fans were noisy. Which was why she'd known the kiln wasn't on. But if Brookshire had turned on the kiln without turning on the fans . . .

Panic fluttered in her throat. She swallowed it away and ran toward the kiln unit. But stopped five feet away, because even that far from it, she could feel the heat reaching out to her.

She heard a faint noise—her own, a sad whimper of fear.

Brookshire had locked her in his kiln and turned it on. How long before it reached peak temperature? How long could she survive in that kind of heat, with no water? Two days? One? Less than that?

"No," she said out loud. She was not going to become a mummified corpse at this point in her life. She was a Moore, and Moores didn't give up. They figured things out.

She used the sleeve of her T-shirt to wipe the sweat from her forehead. No Moore that she'd ever heard of had been trapped in an active lumber kiln, but there'd been one who'd fallen from a tree while deer hunting, broken his leg, and crawled two miles to the nearest road for help.

"Close enough," she murmured.

Phone held high to light her way, she did another walk-through of the kiln, again looking for escape possibilities. The doors opened outward, so there was no chance of unscrewing the hinges, not that she had any tools to do that, but—

She slapped her pants pocket; her Swiss army knife was right there, ready and waiting.

But waiting for what? What could she actually do?

She examined the kiln. If she couldn't figure out anything else, she could use a blade to cut through the wires that powered it. Doing so would send painful 110-volt shocks through her body, but it wouldn't kill her. Probably. She'd still be stuck inside the metal box, though, and getting out mattered more than anything else.

The door wasn't an option. The metal walls were welded together, with double welding at the corners. She ran her hand over every weld she could find, hoping to find something loose or weak, but Brookshire had built the place like a bunker, made to last a hundred years.

What a jerk.

She glanced at her phone's battery readout. Sixty-eight percent? Using the flashlight to inspect the kiln's interior must have taken longer than she realized. She shut down the flashlight, and the space went dark.

What she needed was to think. She sat on the floor, cross-legged, put her elbows on her knees and her chin in her hands, and felt like she was eight years old again, up in the treehouse, back in the days before Lara had come into her life.

But maybe there wasn't a way out.

"No," she said. "There's a way. I just haven't found it yet." Then, since that hadn't sounded confident enough, she shouted it at the top of her lungs. "There's a way!"

Her voice reverberated off the metal walls, back and forth, back and forth. She looked up toward the ceiling, feeling that she could almost see the words bouncing around up there.

But the only thing up there was the vent, so—

The vent.

Slowly, she got to her feet. Her eyes had adjusted to the dark enough for her to know she couldn't reach the vent. But there was a lot of wood in there. Could she pile up enough to reach the vent?

She looked at her hands, soft and uncalloused. "You two are going to be a mess," she told them, and started moving lumber into one great big pile.

Sweat dripped off the end of her nose and ran down her spine. She could feel it being absorbed into her bra, the waistband of her underwear and her socks. It was a remarkably unpleasant thing to feel, but she ignored it and carried on. Literally.

Pick up one end of a piece of wood, drag it down, heave one end up in the air, and lean it against the pile. Climb to the top of the pile, grab the high end, lever it around to be parallel with the rest of the pile, then drag it into place.

She made the pile two planks wide, putting a narrow plank next to a wide one, then on the layer above, putting a wide one next to a narrow one. The idea was that pattern would create a more stable pile for her to stand on, but as it grew in height, she wasn't so sure.

"No choice," she muttered, and kept going. The temperature was rising quickly. Brookshire must have cranked the kiln to the top temperature. She needed to get out of here soon, or she wouldn't have the strength to move.

Pick up, drag, heave, climb, lever, drag.

Pick up, drag, heave, climb, lever, drag.

Pick up, drag, heave, climb, lever, drag.

Over and over and over for so long that Jaime stopped thinking and just worked. Splinters stuck into her hands and arms and even her legs, but she paid no attention. The only thing that mattered was moving wood. The only thing that mattered was getting out of there. Everything else could wait.

She dropped a piece of wood into place on top of the pile and looked up. The vent was just above her head.

Close enough.

She took out her phone and tapped on the flashlight so she could see what kind of screws fastened the fan in place. Phillips. With her other hand, she took out her Swiss army knife, opened the knife's Phillips blade, and undid the screws that held the vent cover in place.

"Righty, tighty; lefty, loosey," she murmured, and one by one, the screws fell away.

She held the vent cover in place with her knife hand, slid her phone into her pants pocket, and used both hands to lower the vent cover.

Then, wondering why she was bothering to be careful, she tossed the metal cover to the floor and almost smiled at the clattering rattle it made on the way down.

Take that, Brookshire.

She shook her head. The heat was starting to turn her brain to mush, and she couldn't afford that.

"Get a grip," she said, and looked up at the fan. Wires, fan blades, and more screws. She eyed it all, then descended to the floor. She picked up the longest wood sticker she could find and carried it to the top of the heap.

Who was it that said, *"Give me a lever and I'll move the world"*? She wasn't sure, but the guy deserved a medal.

Jaime pushed the sticker between the fan blades and leaned. Hard.

The resulting metal screech was an immediate reward. She nodded and kept going. More pushing, more screeching. She wriggled the sticker left and right, loosening the entire fan housing.

She dropped the wood sticker and put her hands on the fan unit. Her breaths were coming fast and shallow. The heat was getting to her. "On three," she panted. "One . . . two . . ." She cheated on herself and pushed.

The fan gave a final metallic screech and tumbled onto the roof. Jaime drank in the small square of blue sky as hot air rushed past her. This would help ease the heat, but it wouldn't save her. And she still needed to actually, you know, get out.

She judged the distance from top of pile to the ceiling as six feet. She needed at least another three feet of height. Back to work.

Pick up, drag, heave, climb, lever, drag.

From the beginning, she'd staggering the plank ends carefully to make a stairway of sorts, but the climb was getting harder and harder.

Pick up, drag, heave, climb, lever, drag.

When she'd put up two layers more of planks than she thought she needed, she took a long breath. It was now or never. If this didn't work, she'd have to sit there and hope for a miracle that almost certainly would never come.

She put her head up through where the vent had been, but her shoulders didn't fit. She tried squishing this way and that. Nothing worked. The hole was too small.

"Do not cry," she murmured. "Do not."

With that settled, she kept contorting herself into different positions, peeling away layer after layer of skin. Nothing. She withdrew, thought a little, then put one arm above her head. This time she slid a little farther, but not enough to get her out.

Huh. If one arm up was good, would two be better?

She took a deep breath, released it to make her ribcage as small as possible and put both arms above her head.

Her arms, head, and shoulders were through. With a whispered "Hallelujah," she placed her palms on the roof and pushed. Her hips got stuck, but that part of her body was rounder and not so solid as her shoulders, and with one last scrape of skin exposed by a rucked-up T-shirt, she pulled her body up onto the roof.

She was out. She was not going to be cooked to a crisp inside Warren Brookshire's kiln.

She was free.

"Thank you," she murmured, and closed her eyes, enjoying the feel of fresh air on her face, and the kind warmth of the sun.

She opened her eyes, turned her head, and met the gaze of Warren Brookshire.

The man, after he'd locked her inside a kiln and turned it on, had gone back to work. He was inside the shop, running a piece of wood through the table saw—Jaime could hear it—and was staring at her, his mouth falling open.

Shock froze her in place. But not for long. The table saw was still cutting wood when she was on the move, slipping and sliding toward the roof's edge. During her up and downing on the wood pile, she'd done the math and judged the roofline as eight feet at the peak, six at the outside edges. A drop of six feet was not going to kill her. All she had to do was get down in one piece and run faster than Brookshire, and she'd be safe.

She reached the roof's edge and lay flat. With both hands, she reached down and flailed around, hunting for something, anything to hang onto.

Her fingertips brushed against the eave's drip edge. It wouldn't take her weight, but there was nothing else, so she grabbed it with both hands and slid her body and feet around. She let herself drop, her fingers losing their grip on the drip edge as her full weight came around. She fell to the grass and tumbled head over heels. Getting up on one knee, superhero style, she shot a quick glance into the shop.

Brookshire was gone. But where was he?

She ran as fast as she could toward her truck, pushing through the scrub and grass, paying no attention to the branches whipping her in the face. She rounded the corner of the shop and slowed.

Brookshire had parked broadside in front of her truck, an inch from her front bumper. She'd backed up to a tree and she didn't have any way to maneuver around his big vehicle. She was completely blocked in. Jumping in and speeding away to safety wasn't an option.

On to plan B.

Which was to run.

So she did. She pumped her arms, pounded her feet, and ran as fast as she could down the driveway. All she had to do was reach the road, then she'd be safe. If she ran into the woods, she might be temporarily safe, but that was no guarantee. She needed to get to town. She'd flag down the first car and convince the driver to—

Something zinged past her ear, quickly followed by a bang. He was shooting at her. Brookshire was shooting at her!

Jaime started zigging and zagging. She had to get to the road, had to—

Zing.

She cried out as fire exploded in her leg.

Bang!

She kept running, but her leg stopped working and she crumpled to the ground. She clambered to her knees, made it to her feet, stood there, swaying.

"You're not going to make it," Brookshire called. "You might as well stop right now."

Jaime gritted her teeth. She would not let this man kill her. *She. Would. Not.* She took one wavery step. Fell down, face and hands in the dirt.

"Aren't you the stubborn one." Brookshire approached, holding a rifle with disturbing familiarity. "Have to say, I didn't expect you to get out of the kiln. Not sure how you got out through that vent, but I bet you damaged it. Wonder if I could bill your estate?"

He tipped his head back and laughed.

Jaime threw the two handfuls of dirt she had gathered up and into his face. Brookshire cursed and stumbled backward, one hand to his eyes, rifle loose in the other. Ignoring the pain in her leg, Jaime leaped forward and yanked the gun away from him. "Back off," she said, pointing the barrel at him.

He smirked. "Oh, please. You really think you're going to shoot me?"

Jaime, who'd been target shooting she was ten and hunting since she was twelve, didn't pause a second. She pulled the trigger and watched the dirt puff up between his feet.

"Back off," she repeated. "Put your hands up."

This time he did what she said.

Just then came the most welcome sound she'd ever heard. A police siren, approaching fast.

She kept the gun trained on Brookshire until the police car, driven by Detective Scoles, bumped its way up the driveway. Kept it on Brookshire until the detective and the deputy ran to her.

"About time you two got here," she said grumpily, handing over the rifle.

Then she fainted.

Chapter
Twenty-Three

A few hours later, after Jaime had been driven in her own truck by Deputy Hoxie to the emergency room—where they'd examined her, bandaged her leg, checked her tetanus booster status, dripped an IV into her, then told her to drink plenty of water, keep an eye on the wound and take it easy for a couple of days—she found herself at the sheriff's office, thanking the office manager for the bottled water that had been forced into her hands.

"Dehydration is no joke," Nicole said, handing over another bottle. "Bax was worried about you."

This surprised Jaime. She'd come out of her annoying faint seconds after she'd fallen, and she'd interpreted the expression on the detective's face as irritation. But she thanked Nicole and let herself be helped along by the elbow to the closest interview room.

"They'll be along in a minute," Nicole said, pulling out a chair for her. "I bet you're hungry. How about a protein bar?"

Jaime demurred, but Nicole didn't pay any attention. And as it turned out, she was right, because, although Jaime ate one of the six to be polite, before she knew it, she'd eaten two and was unwrapping a third when Detective Scoles and Deputy Dave came in.

"Ms. Moore," the detective said, sitting across from her, "how are you feeling?"

Jaime's mouth was full, so she had to chew and swallow before she could talk. "Fine, thanks."

"No ill effects?"

"The doctor said I should take it easy for a day or two. And stay hydrated." To demonstrate that she was following the doctor's orders, she picked up one of the water bottles and took a sip. It tasted so good that she took another. "What happens now?" she asked.

Detective Scoles glanced at the deputy, who was unfolding a lap-top computer. "Now we walk through what happened today. We'll take notes, read them back to you, and ask you to confirm that what we have is correct."

Jaime looked at the diminishing pile of protein bars and wondered if they'd be enough.

As it turned out, they weren't. One hour into their session, after a meaningful glance from the detective, the deputy walked out of the room and returned twenty minutes later with a pile of aluminum foil–wrapped slices of pizza. And more water.

Jaime ate a slice of pepperoni, then kept going, stopping only when one of the men asked for clarification. Finally, when she was out of words, she said, "And that's when you two drove up."

Scoles nodded. "Thank you, Ms. Moore. Do you have any questions for us?"

Of course she did. Starting at the top, she asked, "Why did you drive out there?"

"Your text message," the detective said, frowning. "You do remember sending it, don't you? The photo of the kiln?"

She looked at the table, at her phone, now at one hundred percent thanks to a kind offer from Nicole to lend a charger. "There was hardly any signal. I didn't think the message went out."

Detective Scoles shrugged. "Is that your only question?"

"What is Brookshire saying? This isn't going to be his word against mine, is it? What happens next? Will I have to testify in court? And—"

Scoles held up his hands. "Slow down there. Let's take these one at a time. Deputy, would you like to answer Ms. Moore's first question, about Mr. Brookshire?"

"Yes, sir." Hoxie cleared his throat. "When Mr. Brookshire was first taken into custody, he was saying it was all a huge misunderstanding. He'd assumed you were breaking into his workshop, that perhaps he'd been a little overzealous in pursuing you, but surely we didn't think he'd meant you any real harm."

Jaime went from shock to furious anger in seconds. After she pulled in a long breath, she calmly asked, "How did he explain locking me in the kiln and turning it on?"

"An accident," Deputy Hoxie said. "He's not sure how it happened—he says something like that isn't supposed to happen, but you know how women are, they just don't understand tools."

Jaime had heard that same sentiment over and over. Maybe someday it wouldn't infuriate her, but she hadn't yet reached that point.

"Here." Detective Scoles pushed another piece of pizza toward her. "Eat this. The man is a misogynistic piece of work who wasn't raised right."

"Thanks." Jaime unwrapped the pizza. Ham. She could live with that.

"When we questioned Brookshire about Cilla Price," the deputy said, "telling him we had forensic evidence she'd been in his kiln, he said that was an accident too. That she'd slipped and fallen, hit her head on a rock, and he'd panicked and put her in the kiln."

"An accident? Seriously?" At least that's what Jaime tried to say, but her mouth was full, and her protests came out as muffled mumbles.

"Don't worry," Scoles said. "We know none of that is true."

The deputy nodded. "Besides, how could it be an accident that he kidnapped her from the airport parking lot? There's no way to explain away that fact."

Jaime's irritated anxiety, which had zoomed off the charts, dropped back to normal. And, she learned later, there was no way to explain away the fact that the forensics team had found DNA evidence of Brookshire's presence at her house.

"Here's another interesting fact," Scoles said. "We contacted your ex-husband about the house purchase. He said that soon after he'd purchased it, Mr. Brookshire tried to buy it from him. At that point, however, your ex-husband was planning to have King Contractors renovate it, and said he wasn't interested."

Jaime could easily imagine the conversation. "Let me guess. Henry told him no, Brookshire upped his offer, Henry laughed and said he'd have to double the price, which annoyed Brookshire no end."

The detective gave her a look. "In the room, were you?"

"No," she said tiredly. "But I know Henry, and Brookshire's a lot like him. My guess is he put Cilla's body in the house not because he thought it wouldn't be disturbed for years, but as a sort of punishment to Henry for not selling the house to him."

Detective Scoles eyed her thoughtfully. "Deputy," he said, "make a note of that theory. We'll use that when we question Mr. Brookshire. Thank you, Ms. Moore. Is there anything else you have to add?"

Jaime shook her head. Her story had been told, and there was only one thing she wanted to do. "Can I go?" she asked, her voice embarrassingly small and plaintive.

"Sure," the detective said. "We can contact you later with any further questions. Do you feel up to driving? The deputy here can take you wherever you need to go."

"Thanks, but I'm okay." Jaime stood. "Where I'm going isn't far."

Five minutes later, she pulled into the driveway of her childhood home, and a minute after that, she was inside the comfort of her mother's arms.

* * *

Jaime slept fitfully that night in her old room, her sleep punctuated by dreams of heat and locked doors and being trapped in tiny boxes. She was almost grateful to be rudely awakened by a pillow being thrown at her.

"Really?" she asked, her eyes still closed. "You couldn't have knocked?"

"I did." Lara sat on Jaime's bed, her back against the footboard, her legs stretched out long. Just like old times. "You didn't hear. Speak to me, child. Your text last night was not overly illuminating."

What Jaime had texted was *Brookshire did it. At Mom & Dad's tonight. Talk tomorrow*, which she thought had done an excellent job of covering the basics.

"Not without coffee," she said. A tap on her thigh made her open her eyes. Lara was holding out a steaming mug. "Well, that's more like it." Jaime slid up to a sitting position and took the handle. A few restorative sips later, she started talking.

Two coffee cups later, she came to the end of everything she knew.

"Hmm." Lara squinted at the ceiling. "A few questions. Why was there lumber in the kiln at all? If the lumber was wet, shouldn't the kiln have been working? If it was dry, why was it still in there?"

"Oh. Right." Jaime had, in fact, learned the answer to that. "It was already dried. Brookshire was selling it. That's why he was out there yesterday in the first place, to take pictures to send the guy so they could set the final price."

She'd learned that the grass and scrub had been cleared away from the right side of the shop. The detective had said her trail through the grass on the left side was obvious enough for a toddler to follow.

"So," Lara said. "Bax Scoles wasn't doing such a bad job after all, was he?"

"Nope." Jaime drank the last of her coffee, then waited.

"I suppose I should tell you." Lara sighed. "The reason I was down on him was because way back when, Bax Scoles arrested my brother."

Jaime stared at her friend. Of all the things she'd considered, that hadn't been one of them. "Um. Okay."

"It was a long time ago. Years and years. And I have to admit, my brother kind of deserved it. Anyway, that's why. Back then, I took my brother's side over anyone's, you know?"

Jaime did. Family first. It was the natural order of things.

"Well, I have to get going." Lara slid off the bed. "And your mom's making a bang-up breakfast out there. If you want to shower first, you'd best get rolling."

The previous night, Jaime had taken a long shower to hose off her multiple layers of sweat, but another wouldn't hurt. She got up, gave Lara a huge hug, and was soon in her old seat at the kitchen table. Without asking, her dad poured her another mug of coffee and slid it across the table.

Jaime asked the question she should have asked days ago. "About Roger's law practice. Donna says it's solid. Is that true? Because his office sure doesn't look like it."

Her dad laughed. Her mom, bringing a platter of bacon to the table, said, "That man has more money than all of us Moores put together and tripled."

"He . . . what?"

"Sure," her dad said. "He just hates to spend it."

"He . . . does?"

Her mom put a platter of pancakes on the table and filled Jaime's plate with food. "Roger doesn't spend a dime he doesn't have to, and he makes a boatload. He has clients all over the country coming to him for his expertise in contract law."

"But . . . he charged me hardly anything for my divorce."

"Honey"—Jaime's dad smiled at her—"that's because he's your uncle Roger. Did you think he'd charge you full rate?"

Jaime's shame reddened her face. How could she have gotten things so wrong?

"There's something else that needs saying." Her mother sat down across from her. "About that divorce. I'm sure one of the reasons you've stayed with Lara all these months is because you feel we're disappointed in you for giving up on your marriage, and that's just not true."

"It's . . . not?"

"Far from it," her dad said. "You walked away from something that wasn't good for you."

Her mom reached across the table and took her hand. "You didn't give up. He did. There's a world of difference."

Tears misted Jaime's eyes. She blinked them away. "Thanks," she whispered.

"We should have said all this months ago." Her mom patted her hand. "Sorry it took so long."

"Speaking of revelations," her dad said, grinning, "it was bridge club last night. Want to hear the latest about Arthur King?"

* * *

All through her drive to the house, Jaime couldn't stop laughing. What her dad had told her he'd learned at the card table from a good friend of Arthur King, Henry's father, was that Arthur was *paying* for the pilot of Henry's home renovation show. There was no network looking to make Henry a television star. It was Henry trying to make himself a star with a little bit of help from Natalie and a lot of help from his daddy's money.

"Have at it," Jaime said as she hopped up the porch steps, still laughing. Maybe the show would be a success, and maybe it wouldn't. Either way, she didn't care. Being on television wasn't a goal for her. What mattered was making homes for people, homes that helped make people happy.

Right then, she was pretty happy herself. Warren Brookshire was in jail; her parents didn't think she was a failure; she'd just finished a meeting with Violet Dilworth, her general contractor friend, to use Violet's shop space in exchange for finish carpentry work; and thanks to Roger's lawyering, there might be a chance she'd end up with Brookshire's shop and tools as a settlement in lieu of a lawsuit.

Plus, she'd come up with the perfect place to put the ceramic tuxedo bunny. In walls of bookshelves and cabinets she was going to build in the library, Mr. Rabbit was going to get his own dedicated glass-fronted cubby space. It was his house, after all.

What she needed now was to get the house in good enough shape to get a solid offer. Then she could leverage that into a loan for another house, and then—

"Mmww?"

By this time, Jaime was used to Demo materializing out of nowhere to make figure eights around her ankles. "Well, good morning to you too." Jaime picked him up and snuggled him. "Did you miss me?"

Demo bumped the top of his head against her chin.

"I'll take that as a yes," she said, laughing.

"Well, now," said a male voice, "what a pretty sound, that laugh of yours. I've missed that."

Jaime smiled as Bob McNinch came up the driveway. "Morning," she said. "What brings you out here?"

"Oh, just moseying around." He held out a hand, let Demo sniff it, then scratched the cat under his chin as he gave the house a practiced once-over. "This place is starting to come along, yeah?"

"Getting there." Jaime looked over her shoulder. "Lots to do, but I'm getting there."

"Need any help?"

Her attention jerked from the house to her former foreman. "Bob, I—"

"No, I know you can't bring me in right now. But think about it. You were the brains, heart, and soul behind the success of King Contractors, and you'll be a success with your new business."

She didn't have a new business—not exactly—which she tried to say, but Bob shook his head and kept talking.

"Henry and that Natalie are more tied up with television cameras than working on houses." He shrugged. "Maybe that'll work out for them, maybe it won't. Either way, I'm not interested. I want to fix up houses. And I want to work with you."

Jaime's mind was already made up. This was something she'd been considering for days. "Sorry, Bob," she said shaking her head. "I don't want you to work for me." She grinned. "How about a partnership?"

*   *   *

An hour later, Jaime waved good-bye to Bob. They'd hammered out a tentative deal, and she'd called Roger and asked him to draw up the paperwork. He'd said they could come in midweek to review.

Bob and his wife, as she'd suspected for years, were savers not spenders, and they were willing to invest a significant amount of their cash into the business that would be called Momentum Construction.

"I believe," Jaime said to the tailgate of Bob's receding truck, "that this is going to work out just fine."

"Glad to hear it." The lilac bushes rustled, and Mike Darden emerged, two coffees in hand.

"You keep on doing this and we're going to end up with a permanent path between our houses," she said, taking the cup he was offering.

"Would that be such a bad thing?" His smile was deep, kind, and magnetic.

Feeling its pull, she took a slow step toward him. "Might be a really good thing."

"What I was thinking."

"I value your friendship," she said softly.

"Back at you," he said just as softly.

"But I just got divorced."

He nodded. "Heard about that."

"And I want to get it out there that, um . . ." She searched for words that wouldn't make her feel like an idiot, because maybe she'd been reading him all wrong. Maybe he didn't have any interest in her, romance-wise. "So that you know what's going on with me. I'm not ready to be anything other than friends with anyone. At least for a little while. I don't want anyone to be my rebound."

"Okay," he said, and his kind eyes were the only things she could see. "I don't suppose you have a definition of what 'a little while' means, do you?"

"Not yet. I'll probably start working on it soon, though."

"Okay," he said again. "How will I know when you finish it?"

She took a sip of coffee and considered her answer. "Guess you'll just have to wait and see," she said to the plastic lid.

Then she looked straight at him.

And smiled.

Acknowledgments

Thanks so very, very much to my fellow PlotHatchers—Ginger Bolton, Peg Cochran, Krista Davis, Kaye George, Daryl Wood Gerber, and Marilyn Levinson. I couldn't have done this without you.